Megan's Big Surprise

Suddenly, I couldn't help blurting out, "I may have some big news, too, pretty soon."

Of course, everyone wanted to know what my big news was.

"It's a surprise," I said. "Only Daphne knows what it is."

"You won't even tell *me,* Megan?" Mom sounded hurt and I felt glad.

My sisters kept pestering me, wanting to know what my surprise was. But of course I wouldn't tell them.

I wouldn't tell anyone until tryouts were over and I could brag, too—about getting the part of Princess Leyla in the play.

It was all I could do not to shout, "Move over, gorgeous Gina and brilliant Brenda. Make way for marvelous Megan!"

Don't Get Mad, Get Even!

Don't Get Mad, Get Even!

Rona S. Zable

Published by Troll Associates, Inc.
Rainbow Bridge is an imprint of Troll Associates.

Printed in the United States of America.

10 9 8 7 6 5 4 3 2 1

For my niece,
Lori Shuster Brown

Don't Get Mad, Get Even!

Chapter 1

"*Another* housekeeper quit?" Jeremy's mouth dropped open. "What happened?"

"Mrs. Feeney has gone off to greener pastures," I said.

He gave me a knowing look. "Yeah, right, Megan. What'd you pull this time?"

"I didn't pull anything—honest. She quit before I had a chance."

I told Jeremy what happened. In the middle of breakfast on Saturday morning, Mrs. Feeney yanked off her apron, kicked the stove, and announced that she had lined up a better job with some rich people in Newton.

Her parting words were: "I'm goin' off to greener pastures."

Later my father joked that this was quite fitting, since Mrs. Feeney ate like a horse anyhow.

Even after he heard my story, Jeremy was certain I had something to do with Mrs. Feeney leaving. I guess my reputation keeps following me. "Wow. That makes six housekeepers so far." He stared at me in awe. "And you got rid of all of them."

Like I said, I really can't take 100 percent credit for Mrs. Feeney. It's true I got her all nervous when I made up that story about our house being haunted by the ghost of a housekeeper who had been murdered years back. "It happened right here in the kitchen," I told her in a low voice. "I'm not supposed to talk about it."

But what really did Mrs. Feeney in was our electric stove. She hated it. "I can't cook decent on them electric things," she complained. "I like a gas stove. I'll take gas any day."

She kept burning the eggs, and that's what finally made her snap. Oh, I admit I helped things along by asking for fried eggs every morning, even though I don't really like them. It was those last two eggs—sunny-side up and slightly burned—that pushed Mavis Feeney over the edge.

"Where does your mother keep finding all those housekeepers?" Jeremy wanted to know.

"Beats me," I said. "She never gives up. In fact, there's another new one starting today."

It was a windy afternoon late in February, and I was out of breath from trying to keep up with Jeremy as we walked home from school. He's a lot taller than I am, and he's skinny.

Behind us I heard a familiar and very annoying sound—a cross between a snort and a snicker. I would recognize that sound *anywhere*. It could belong to only one person—my next-door neighbor, Vonna Mae Peckham.

I've known Vonna since kindergarten. Even then she was a pill, with her blond banana curls and that loud voice of hers, bragging about how she was going to take baton-twirling lessons so she could be in the Miss America Pageant when she grew up.

In second grade Vonna started calling me Chubs. Later on her dumb older brother, Bart, gave me the nickname Mega-Brat Megan.

But I didn't get mad at them. Instead I got *even!*

I gave them nicknames, too—Vomit and Barf. That shut *them* up!

Today Vonna was with her friend, Saralee, a Vonna clone with carrot-red hair. The two of them were whispering and giggling in back of us. Saralee had even gotten a curly perm so she could look more like Vonna, and she'd started taking baton-twirling lessons, too. I guess Saralee was planning to be first runner-up when Vonna became Miss America.

"Oh, Saralee," Vonna trilled, "you'll never guess who signed up for the play tryouts. Megan Dooley. Can you believe it?"

I gritted my teeth and tried to ignore them.

Except for Jeremy, who's my best friend, I didn't think anybody else knew I had signed up for tryouts.

Our class play is a really big event at school. This year we're putting on a comedy called *The Magic House.* It's about this princess who doesn't want to go through with the marriage that's been arranged for her because she's sure the prince will be a nerd. His hobby is magic and he gives performances in disguise as Marvello the Magician. Anyhow, Princess Leyla calls on her fairy godmother, Klutzella, to help her, but Klutzella is a real ditz and keeps losing her magic powers. The plot is kind of complicated, but it really is funny.

I've never wanted anything as much as I wanted the part of Princess Leyla. I like acting, and I knew I'd be good in the part, even though I haven't been in a school play since fourth grade, two years ago. Back then I had the part of Pocahontas, but I came down with the flu the day of the play and never got a chance to show people I could act.

Jeremy thinks the reason I want to be Princess Leyla is because Randy Howard will probably get the part of Marvello the Magician, and there's a scene at the end where Marvello kisses the princess and breaks the spell.

Randy always gets the lead whenever there's a school play. His mother is the director of the

Winslow Community Theater, and Randy's been acting since he was a little kid.

I would never admit it, but I certainly wouldn't mind being kissed by Randy Howard. Every girl in our class has a crush on him.

There was more whispering behind us. Then Saralee said loudly, "Oh, Vonna, what part do you think Megan should try out for in *The Magic House?*"

"Well, I think Megan would be just perfect as . . . the *house*!" Vonna shrieked, and the two of them collapsed in giggles.

I whirled around to face them. "Why don't you go twirl your batons," I snapped.

"Now, now, Megan," Vonna said sweetly. "We were only kidding. Don't get mad."

"Oh, you know me, Vonna," I said. "I don't get mad—I get *even.*"

That must have made Vonna nervous because she decided to stop at Saralee's house. After the two of them left, the walk home was a lot more pleasant.

Jeremy and I live in what they call the old section of Winslow, Massachusetts. It has all these big, historic houses that have been fixed up and modernized. I think it's a lot nicer than the newer section of town. The only thing I don't like is that the houses are built very close together. That means I have to deal with Vonna living next door.

Jeremy asked if I wanted to go over to his house, since we didn't have much homework. "We could play some telephone tricks," he suggested.

I considered it, then changed my mind. Jeremy's whole family is into computers. Both his parents work at home, and they're always at their terminals, clicking away. Whenever I visit there, I feel like I'm on a spaceship.

"Some other time," I said. "Let's go to my house instead and check out the new housekeeper."

As we neared my house, I saw Mom's van in the driveway.

"Uh-oh." Jeremy chuckled. "I guess your mother wants to make sure you don't scare away the new housekeeper."

"Yeah," I agreed. "Otherwise Mom would never be home in the afternoon."

Nothing's been right since Mom started her own business last year. She thought up this personal service called Let Mama Do It—Mama, of course, being her. The idea caught on and suddenly she was away all the time, doing chores and errands for everyone—sewing on buttons, cleaning closets, planning birthday parties, stuff like that.

In fact, Mom was so busy she didn't have time to sew buttons on *our* clothes, or clean *our* closets. Mom even forgot my sister Brenda's birthday. She was too busy planning a birthday party for some bratty little kid who wouldn't even let Mom have a piece of his cake.

Mom would drive people to the airport, look in on old folks whose relatives lived out of town, even arrange family reunions. She had some weird clients, too, like Fanny Gunkel, who used to call our house at all hours of the night because she couldn't sleep and wanted Mom to talk to her.

Nobody in my family was thrilled about Mom's business, but they didn't seem to mind as much as I did.

Dad is an accountant, and he said that all the publicity about Mom brought him new clients.

My two sisters didn't complain much. Gina, my older sister, is sixteen and busy with her cheerleading. Brenda, my younger sister, who's ten, was busy getting straight A's.

And then there was me, in the middle of Beauty and Brains, with no special talent, and not very busy with anything, unless you count my telephone tricks. I really missed having Mom around. I missed those after-school talks and the games of Scrabble and just knowing she was there.

Mom said she didn't want the house to get neglected, so she hired a cleaning service twice a week. And then she asked Great-Aunt Maybelle to come live with us and keep an eye on my sisters and me. Except Aunt Maybelle kept her eyes on the TV set. She's a TV-talk-show junkie.

But even though there was somebody in the house and things were getting vacuumed and dusted, there was still the problem of cooking and cleaning up, not to mention laundry and ironing. That's when Mom decided we needed a live-in housekeeper.

Can you imagine what our house was like then? I mean, there's Gina, practicing her cheers in the basement; Brenda, cluttering up the kitchen table with her science projects; Aunt Maybelle with her eyes glued to a blaring television set day and night; clients calling both my parents—plus a crabby, old housekeeper creeping around and yelling at us.

I mean, it was like Visitors' Day at the State Hospital!

Somebody had to get rid of those house-keepers. I figured it was up to me. That way Mom was bound to come to her senses and realize she would simply have to cut down on her hours. Then maybe things would be the way they used to be.

"Maybe your new housekeeper is baking cookies," Jeremy said hopefully.

"Could be," I said, taking out my back-door key. "Aldora Hicks did that the first day to make a good impression."

But there was nothing baking and nobody bustling around the kitchen. Instead I heard voices in the living room.

Then and there, I knew there was something different about *this* housekeeper.

Nobody ever sits in our living room. Not since Mom had the sofa and chairs reupholstered in oyster white.

So imagine my surprise to see Mom actually sitting on a chair in the forbidden living room. Perched on the white sofa was Aunt Maybelle. She was talking with a woman who was obviously Housekeeper Number Seven.

Jeremy stood hesitantly in the hallway, but I marched right in.

"Oh, hello there, Megan." Mom looked up and smiled brightly. "There's somebody I want you to meet. Daphne, this is my middle daughter, Megan."

It came out sounding like a sigh.

"And Megan," Mom said almost pleadingly, "this is our new housekeeper, Daphne Winston."

Translation: Megan, please don't pull any of your tricks. Be nice.

"Ah—so this is Megan. I'm delighted to meet you." Daphne Winston had a rich, theatrical voice that sounded like she ought to be playing Shakespeare rather than cleaning house.

That's probably why Mom hired her. That high-class voice would certainly impress any client who might call our house.

I sized Daphne up quickly. She certainly didn't

resemble any of the previous housekeepers. Mildred Coombs, Sophie Nokemura, and Laverne Hopwood wore uniforms. Aldora Hicks wore pink pantsuits that matched the pink sponge curlers in her hair. Ella Tinkham wore flowered house-dresses, and Mavis Feeney clumped around in a stained butcher apron over her baggy slacks.

Daphne Winston was dressed like she was going to a party instead of cleaning house. She had on a ruffled blouse, a longish skirt, and leather boots with high heels. Her dark hair was piled high on her head, and her blue eyes were fringed with false eyelashes that looked like little brushes. She had long, dangling earrings that clinked when she moved her head. In her hand was a big feather duster.

I had to admit Daphne was better looking than the others, but that wasn't difficult. Also, she was a lot younger.

But the agency must have been running out of housekeepers for us. They were practically scraping the bottom of the barrel.

Daphne Winston was a pushover, I decided. I could get rid of her in two days. Three at the most.

She smiled and held out her hand to me. "Your mother was telling me how bright you are, Megan."

Translation: Your mother already warned me about you.

Daphne looked over at Jeremy, who was standing in the doorway, taking everything in. "And who is this charming young man?"

"That's my friend, Jeremy Simpson," I said, emphasizing the word "friend." I didn't want her to think Jeremy was my boyfriend. He's my pal and that's all.

"Jeremy Simpson!" Daphne repeated his name in that musical voice of hers, rolling it around on her tongue so it sounded as if Jeremy Simpson was some kind of celebrity. "Well, Jeremy, it certainly is a pleasure to meet you, too."

He looked positively dazzled. I couldn't believe the way he kept staring at Daphne with his mouth hanging open.

Mom glanced at her watch. "Oh, dear, I have to take the Lawrence boy to the orthodontist. But I did want to make sure you were getting along all right." She looked at Daphne's outfit and cleared her throat. "Er—don't you think you'd find it easier to work in something more comfortable?"

"Why, yes, you're absolutely right," Daphne said, staring at her clothing as if she were seeing it for the first time. "It's just that I didn't want to look like a frump."

Mom smiled and stood up. "Well, before I leave, I thought it would be nice to have a cup of tea," she said pointedly. "What do you think, Daphne?"

The new housekeeper nodded. "Oh, yes, I'd love some. One sugar and just a splash of milk, please."

"Well, I certainly didn't mean . . . that is, I thought *you* would make the . . . oh, never mind." Mom turned to Aunt Maybelle. "Would you put on some tea, Auntie?"

Mom left the room with Aunt Maybelle scampering behind her. Daphne settled herself more comfortably on the sofa, obviously in no great hurry to do any housekeeping.

I was confused. Was Daphne dumb or smart or what? She didn't seem to have a clue about being a housekeeper.

"Sit down, Megan." She patted the sofa cushion next to her. "Tell me about your day at school."

My day at school? I couldn't remember the last time anyone had asked about my day at school. Not since Mom went off to her Brilliant Career.

Before I could say anything, Jeremy blurted out, "Megan is getting all hyper about tryouts for the class play."

"Oh, are you interested in acting, Megan?" Daphne's face lit up. "That's wonderful."

"Yeah, but see, Megan wants the lead in the play," Jeremy went on. "Only there's this girl—Vonna—and everyone figures she'll get the lead because she's pretty and—"

I glared at Jeremy and he shut up. Honestly, that guy may be smart in school, but in real life, his blades need sharpening! Why did he have to mention anything about Vonna being pretty? That was especially annoying, since I have mud-brown hair and I'm kind of chunky.

Daphne looked at me thoughtfully. "Well, I think Megan will do very nicely at tryouts. She has strong presence and an interesting voice."

"She *does?"* Jeremy looked astonished.

"I do?" I was astonished, too.

"I tend to be aware of such things," Daphne said. "It so happens I'm a professional actress myself."

"An actress?" I echoed. No wonder she had that terrific voice. "You mean like on Broadway?"

"On Broadway and off Broadway," Daphne answered. "Summer stock, television, you name it. I've even taught speech and drama workshops."

"Then how come you're working as a housekeeper?" Jeremy asked.

Daphne sighed. "How come indeed. Let's just say I am at a crossroads in life. I have to decide between career and marriage. And meantime," she added ruefully, "one must eat, of course."

"I saw this real neat play last year," Jeremy babbled, blushing like crazy. "I was visiting my grandparents and they took me to a play called *Our Town*."

"That's one of my favorite plays, too," Daphne said with a smile. "I've played Emily many times."

Just then Aunt Maybelle appeared in the doorway. "Tea's ready, Daffy."

"It's *Daphne*," she corrected. I smothered a giggle and tried to catch Jeremy's eye, but he wouldn't look at me.

Daphne stood up gracefully. I noticed she had really good posture and walked exactly the way you'd expect an actress to walk.

Aunt Maybelle offered us tea, but Jeremy and I didn't want any. I took a box of cinnamon graham crackers into the den so we could have a snack while we watched television.

I was surprised to see my sister, Brenda, sitting on the sofa, her eyes fastened to the TV screen. Brenda hardly ever watches TV. She's usually studying or doing a project for extra credit.

"What are you watching, Bren?" I asked as I flopped down next to her.

She was busy taking notes and motioned me to be quiet. Out of the corner of her mouth, she whispered, "This is a special science program about cracks in the earth's surface."

"Oh, wow. We wouldn't want to miss *that,*" I said.

Jeremy and I watched the program, quietly munching on graham crackers. When it was over, Brenda promptly shut off the set. She's never been one to waste time watching afternoon television.

"Hey, don't run off," I said. "Talk to us. What do you think of Daffy Duck, our new housekeeper?"

Brenda pursed her lips. "Daphne seems quite intelligent," she said.

That was a typical Brenda comment. She judges people by how smart she thinks they are.

"Oh, get real," I said. "It's that theatrical voice of hers. That's why Daphne sounds intelligent."

"What does it matter what I think of her, anyway? You'll get rid of Daphne just like you got rid of all the others."

Jeremy, who had been sitting there stuffing his face with crackers, suddenly spoke up. "Daphne's different from the others."

"Oh, she's different, all right." I rolled my eyes to the ceiling. "Different, as in weird, ditzy, or off the wall—"

"Well, I really like Daphne," Jeremy said stubbornly.

"Oh, sure. You just like her because she called you charming."

Jeremy's face turned red. "She's nice."

"That's easy for *you* to say, Jeremy," I snapped. "Your mother works at home. My mother's never home anymore. And as long as there's a housekeeper around, Mom will be off doing things for everyone else when we need her here."

"That's not the only reason you don't want a

housekeeper." Brenda sniffed. "You're mad because the housekeeper took my room and I had to move into your room. You know you hate it."

"Of course I hate it," I said. "Who wouldn't? You stay up late studying, you talk to yourself, you make those disgusting noises in your sleep—"

"Well, I happen to agree with Jeremy," Brenda cut in. "I like Daphne, too. She's different." With that, Brenda gathered up her notes and marched upstairs.

I flicked the TV set back on, but I couldn't seem to keep my mind on the programs.

Something kept nagging at me. Something about Daphne. It was true, she certainly *was* different from the other housekeepers. But what of it? And what did it have to do with me?

Jeremy gave me a sour glance. "Why do you have that funny look on your face, Megan? Are you figuring out how to get rid of Daphne?"

"Are you kidding? I won't have to do a thing," I told him loftily. "She'll probably trip on those high-heeled boots. Or get her dangling earrings caught in the garbage disposal." I grinned.

"Daphne Winston," I said, "is a piece of cake. And a *fruitcake* at that!"

Chapter 2

After Jeremy went home, I felt restless, so I decided to play some telephone tricks before dinner.

Telephone tricks aren't easy to do anymore—not with a housekeeper around. There's just no privacy. I have to sneak in my phone calls whenever I can. I went upstairs to my parents' bedroom so I could use the special phone Mom has for her business.

I quickly dialed a number I knew by heart. "Hello, is this Randy Howard?" I cleared my throat. "This is *Seventeen* magazine calling. We're doing a survey and we'd like to ask you a few questions."

"Is this for real?" Randy wanted to know.

"It won't take long," I went on hurriedly. "We want to know what qualities boys look for in a girl. Question number one: What kind of girl do you like? Someone who's pretty? Someone who's popular? Someone who's funny?"

"Yes," said Randy. He sure isn't the easiest person to do a survey on.

I tried another tactic. "Question number two: Is there any special girl you like right now and—"

"Hey, wait a minute," Randy said. "I recognize your voice. I think I know who this is."

"Thank you for your time, Mr. Howard," I said, and slammed down the receiver. Darn. If only Randy hadn't recognized my voice, maybe I could have found out who he liked.

Downstairs Daphne was tinkling a dinner bell. I couldn't believe it. Where had she gotten that? I washed up and went down to the kitchen.

"Dinner's not quite ready," Daphne told me breathlessly. "Give me a few more minutes."

I watched as she raced around the kitchen, running from the table to the stove, dumping salt and pepper into a big pot which she would stir now and then.

The other housekeepers had looked like they were cooking. Daphne looked like a mad scientist doing an experiment.

"Hey," I said, glancing around the table, "where is everyone tonight? There are only three places set."

"Oh, it's going to be just Brenda, you, and me," Daphne explained. "Gina is over at her friend's house, Aunt Maybelle has her Tuesday Club, and both your parents are working late."

I sat down at the table and watched Daphne some more. I noticed she wasn't wearing those fancy high-heeled boots. Now she had on high-top sneakers and a frilly apron over her skirt and blouse.

"Hey, what's burning?" Brenda asked as she joined us.

"Burning? Oh, dear!" Daphne scurried over to the stove and shut it off. She scraped the bottom of the pot, took a taste with the spoon, then stuck the spoon right back in the pot. I hate it when people do that. It's so unsanitary.

"The top is fine," she announced happily. "It's only burned at the bottom."

Daphne spooned the glop into a bowl and put it in front of me. She also brought over a platter of chicken.

I took a piece of chicken and cut into it. Pink juice ran out. Ugh! There's nothing more disgusting than chicken that hasn't been cooked through. Daphne apologized and put the chicken back in the oven.

"Megan, while you're waiting for the chicken, try the ratatouille," Daphne said, pointing to the bowl full of mushy vegetables in a watery red sauce.

"Ratty what?" I asked. "What do you call this stuff?"

"Oh, you're so dumb," Brenda informed me

in her know-it-all voice. “Ratatouille is a French word. It’s a dish that’s made with eggplant and squash and stuff.”

I took a mouthful, and it was as if my tongue had been set on fire. Tears came to my eyes. I grabbed my glass of water and drank it down in one gulp. I tried to tell Daphne she had put in way too much pepper, only I couldn’t talk.

“We had that word in the championship spelling bee,” Brenda said. “I can spell it,” she added smugly. “R-A-T-A—”

“Maybe you can spell it,” I managed to gasp, “but I bet you can’t eat it!”

Brenda didn’t pay any attention to me. She took a forkful, put it in her mouth, then started to cough and choke. I swear, I think I saw steam coming out of her nose.

Daphne kept apologizing. “I’m so sorry. I’m afraid I was a bit nervous, this being my first meal and all.”

Brenda just sat there in silence. I could tell she was mad. Not me. Like I always say, I don’t get mad—I get even.

When Mom got home, I intended to give her a full report about Daphne’s disgusting dinner.

Around eight-thirty, I heard Mom’s car pull into the driveway.

I had a lot to tell her. Not only about Daphne

but about the play, too. I hadn't gotten a chance to tell Mom about the tryouts yet. Maybe she could give me some tips on how to read my lines.

But Mom was in no mood to talk. "I've never been so exhausted," she groaned, kicking off her shoes and flopping down on the sofa in the den. "No sooner did I drive the Andersons to the airport when Bernice remembered she'd left her makeup case at home. So I had to rush back, get the makeup, and bring it to the airport. I got there five minutes before their plane took off."

"You should have phoned to let us know you'd be late," Dad said. "I was getting worried."

"Oh, honey, I'm sorry." Mom patted his hand. "You're right. It's just that I didn't even have a minute to make a phone call. It won't happen again, I promise."

"I've heard that song before," Dad said, but he was smiling. He can never stay mad at Mom for long.

I broke into the conversation. "Hey, Mom, I want to tell you about—"

"Megan, please, not right now." She ran a hand across her forehead. "I want to catch my breath. Let me unwind, sweetie."

I sat around for a few more minutes, waiting for her to unwind and then ask how Daphne was doing and how things were going. But instead, Mom started telling Dad about some new client who wanted Mom to attend a parent-teacher conference because she was too busy to go herself.

"Can you imagine?" Mom clucked. "Her own child and she's too busy to go to a parent-teacher conference."

I wanted to remind Mom that she had missed *my* parent-teacher conference because she'd been delayed doing errands for cranky Mr. Gerber.

Mom turned to me with a tired smile. "Oh, I'm so beat tonight, Megan. But I'll try to get home earlier tomorrow. We'll talk then, all right? Unless it's something important . . ." Her voice trailed off.

"No, it's all right," I mumbled. "It's not that important."

It seemed as if nothing I had to say was very important anymore.

I had just finished brushing my teeth when I heard the weirdest sound coming from Daphne's room.

As I stood outside her half-closed door, I could hear Daphne chanting, over and over, *"Guns and drums—drums and guns."*

Without thinking I pushed open the door and burst into the room. "What's going on?" I cried.

Daphne was in her bathrobe in front of the mirror. She turned around and smiled at me.

"Oh, hello there, Megan. I was just practicing my voice exercises."

I must have looked baffled because she went on. "What you do is, you take a deep breath and sound out the words in one pitch. *Guns and drums—drums and guns.* Like that."

"What's that supposed to do?" I asked.

"It makes the quality of the voice richer and deeper," Daphne replied.

"It does?" That made me think. If my voice had sounded deeper, I might have been able to fool Randy Howard when I phoned him earlier. "Would that exercise work for *my* voice?"

"Oh, yes. It's very effective. And so is the one I call the Magic Exercise. You put a consonant in front of all the vowels and speak slowly. Like this."

Daphne took a deep breath. *"Bay, baw, bee, bye, boy, boo, bow, bah.* Now you try it."

I did. I had to admit it *did* make my voice sound deeper and stronger. I sat down on the edge of her bed, amazed.

She showed me some other exercises and told me about the speech and voice workshops she used to conduct. "I majored in theater arts at college," Daphne said, "and I've taught drama classes."

Suddenly it came to me. An idea that was positively electrifying!

Daphne Winston was a professional actress.

She had appeared on Broadway and on television. She had taught speech and voice workshops and drama classes . . .

And she could give me acting lessons!

With Daphne's coaching I could beat out Vonna Mae for the part of Princess Leyla. For once, my parents would be able to brag about me, too, the way they always seemed to brag about my sisters.

I jumped up from the bed. "Daphne," I cried excitedly, "I want you to give me acting lessons." I tried to explain how important it was to me.

Daphne didn't answer right away. Finally she said, "I'd be willing to give you acting lessons on one condition. You'd have to do something for me in return."

"Okay. Like what?"

"Well," Daphne began, "I know I'm not the world's greatest housekeeper . . ."

I bit back a smart remark.

"And so," she continued, "I could use your help now and then—clearing the table, straightening up, taking out the garbage."

I couldn't believe my ears. Me *helping* a housekeeper? After getting rid of all the other ones?

There was a long silence. "All right," I said, swallowing hard, "it's a deal." I wanted the lead in the play so badly I would do just about anything.

"But I don't want anyone in my family to know about the lessons," I added. "I want to surprise them when I get the lead."

That was one of the best parts of my electrifying idea. In a few weeks, I would come home and mention—ever so casually—that I was going to be Princess Leyla in the school play. Everyone would be so surprised, and Mom would ask how come I'd never even told her I was trying out for the lead. And I would answer—ever so sweetly—that I had *tried* to tell her, but she'd been too busy to listen.

That would make Mom feel guilty for sure.

"All right," Daphne agreed. "Then I'll plan on giving you lessons right before dinner when nobody's around." She held out her hand. "Deal?"

"Deal," I said grimly. We shook hands.

I couldn't believe this was actually happening. For once, I was *not* going to get rid of a housekeeper.

Not Daphne Winston. Not yet.

Not till after tryouts!

Chapter 3

"Is this Mr. Wilfred Boggs?" I took a deep breath the way Daphne had showed me. "This is the radio quiz show, *You Bet Your Boots* calling. If you can answer our jackpot question, you'll win the grand prize."

It was the following Tuesday, and I had stopped at Jeremy's house after school to play some telephone tricks. We had picked the name of Wilfred Boggs out of the phone book.

"Oh, my goodness!" Wilfred Boggs sounded kind of old, but he seemed very happy that somebody was calling him.

"All right, now here is the jackpot question. Name two of the seven dwarfs in *Snow White.* You've got ten seconds, Mr. Boggs."

"Snoopy!" he cried. "No, no—I mean Sneezy."

"Six seconds. Five seconds."

"It's on the tip of my—*Dopey!* That's it—Dopey." He sounded so thrilled I felt guilty.

"Well, congratulations to you, Mr. Wilfred Boggs. You have answered the jackpot question." Jeremy, who was standing nearby, clapped loudly.

"What did I win?" Mr. Boggs asked excitedly.

"Wilfred Boggs," I announced dramatically, "your grand prize is one bucket of fresh horse manure! Would you like to try for *two* buckets?"

With that I started to giggle and hung up the phone. Jeremy was laughing his head off.

I don't like to brag, but I'm really good at playing tricks on the telephone. I mean, it's a *gift*. Sometimes I put on a thick accent, or pretend I'm conducting a survey and ask all kinds of personal questions. You'd be surprised what people will tell you on the telephone.

One of the best tricks I played was back in fifth grade when I fooled Vonna Mae. I put on an accent and said I was calling from the Lorelei Photo Studio. I said that she had been chosen as "Most Beautiful Fifth Grader" and had won a free color photo. I told her to come to the studio Saturday morning at eleven-thirty. Vonna fell for it.

That Saturday Jeremy and I went to the mall to see if Vonna would show up. Sure enough, along came Vonna and her mother, right on schedule. They were all dressed up and they strutted into the studio. A few minutes later, they came rushing out. Mrs. Peckham's face was as red as a beet, and Vonna was yelling and crying. Jeremy and I watched the whole thing from Kinney Shoes next door, laughing like crazy.

"Let's see," I said. "Who else could we call?"

"Not Randy Howard." Jeremy had a mean smile on his face. "I heard that his mother got an unlisted number because Randy was getting too many phone calls from girls."

I ignored that. It so happened that I already knew about the unlisted number. I'd found out about it when I tried to phone Randy a few days earlier. "Let's call Vonna. She's been a real pain lately."

Vonna's brother, Bart, answered the phone and said she wasn't home yet from her tap-dancing lessons. This was another new activity. Now Vonna could tap and twirl her way into everyone's hearts in the talent competition at the Miss America Pageant.

But as I spoke to Bart, I realized something new and different was happening.

Bart hadn't recognized my voice. He always does.

"Well, then, may I talk to your mother, please?" I said. I was speaking in a lower register, projecting my voice.

"One sec. Hey, Ma, it's for you," Bart yelled.

Mrs. Peckham came to the telephone. She

sounded mean and crabby. Vonna and Bart must take after her.

"Pardon me," I said, taking a deep breath, "but are you the lady who washes?"

"Certainly not," Mrs. Peckham snapped.

"Well, then, you must be pretty *dirty* by now." With that, I slammed down the receiver.

Jeremy, who had been listening on the extension, came into the kitchen, laughing. "You sure fooled her."

"Yeah, and I even fooled Bart. He usually recognizes my voice right away."

Jeremy stared at me, puzzled. "How did you do that?"

"Do what?"

"Whatever it is you did with your voice. It sounded so different, like you were older or somebody else or something. How'd you do it?"

"Did I really sound that different?" I was thrilled.

So thrilled that I decided to let Jeremy in on my little secret. "Daphne's been giving me acting lessons. She's teaching me voice exercises and breathing and stuff."

I didn't tell Jeremy that in return I had been helping Daphne around the house. That would have been too humiliating.

"Oh, so Daphne's giving you acting lessons, huh? I should have figured something was going on. No wonder you're being nice to her."

"I am *not* being nice to her," I corrected him. "I'm just not trying to get rid of her, that's all. Not until after tryouts."

He shook his head. "You sure are rotten, Megan."

I ignored that remark. "I've been practicing these voice exercises every chance I can get. Oh, and Daphne says humming is very good, too. If you hum in a monotone, it gives your voice resonance. Try this—take a deep breath, and while you're humming, breathe out through your nose."

Jeremy tried it. "Too bad I didn't know this exercise back in third grade," he said and we both started to laugh.

That's how the two of us got to be friends. Back in third grade, Jeremy was a shy, skinny, little kid with straw-colored hair and glasses. He had this squeaky little voice, and the kids in our class used to make fun of him. They called him Mouse. One day when they were teasing him, I got so mad I said I'd punch out anyone who called him Mouse again. From then on, nobody picked on him and we've been buddies.

"Hey, I'm hungry," Jeremy said. "Want something to eat?"

"What've you got?" There's never anything good to eat at Jeremy's house. Besides computers, his parents are also into health food. The only snacks they seem to have are raw vegetables and organic figs.

Jeremy rummaged around in the refrigerator and took out a container. "Oh, good—cauliflower and red peppers. Want some?"

I made a face.

"Red peppers have more vitamin C than oranges," he told me indignantly. "And they're not cheap either. They cost $3.99 a pound this week."

"Thanks anyhow, but I have to get home. Daphne is supposed to give me a lesson later on. We have to sneak them in because I don't want anyone in my family to know I'm trying out for the play. They'll flip when they find out I got the lead."

I put on my jacket and walked home. One thing you can say about my house—there's plenty to eat, and not just cauliflower and red peppers, either. Ever since Aunt Maybelle came to live with us, we've become junk-food junkies.

Aunt Maybelle loves sweets. Most ladies her age are little old ladies. Aunt Maybelle is a *big* old lady—big and fat. Her face is so round it looks like someone drew it with a compass. Her white hair is cut in little wisps and points like a pixie, and it makes her look like an old elf.

"Teatime, Megan," Aunt Maybelle called out gaily as I came in.

Afternoon tea was something Aunt Maybelle had suggested after she learned that Daphne had lived in London for a year when she was in a play there. Aunt Maybelle had always wanted to know what a real British afternoon tea was like. She just loves anything that's British. She even subscribes to *Royalty* magazine.

Actually, I'd come to the decision that afternoon tea wasn't such a bad idea. I would stuff myself so much that I didn't feel like eating dinner.

This was just as well, since Daphne still wasn't much of a cook, except for things like tomato soup or grilled cheese sandwiches or hamburgers. Her housekeeping wasn't much better than her cooking, although she really did try.

As usual, my parents were so busy they didn't even notice. They had both been working late the past week. Mom was busy with her clients and Dad was busy doing income taxes.

I went into the kitchen where Aunt Maybelle was ringing Daphne's little china dinner bell. "Teatime everyone, teatime." Auntie was in her glory, rinsing out the teapot, cutting crusts off the bread, and piling sweets on the tray. She insisted on using the good bone china teacups. We had already broken three of them.

I was surprised to see Brenda come racing into the kitchen. I guess she liked this afternoon tea business, too.

"Maybelle, dear. We might want something a little lighter," Daphne said gently. She put some thin cucumber sandwiches on a plate and set out cut-up fruit. "After all, we don't want to lose our girlish figures, do we?"

As we sipped our tea, Aunt Maybelle got on her favorite subject, the British royal family. For some reason, she had the idea that anyone who lived in London for a year was probably on close terms with the royals.

Then again, maybe I put a bug in her ear by telling her that Daphne had been on the same bowling team as Prince Charles. I don't know why I *do* things like that.

"Tell me, Daphne," Aunt Maybelle leaned forward and said in a confidential whisper. "Do you think Gertie dyed her hair?"

"Gertie? Who's Gertie?" Daphne asked, puzzled.

"Oh, you know. Gertie—the one with the red hair who was married to Prince Charles's brother."

"You mean Fergie," Daphne said. "Sarah Ferguson—she was married to Prince Andrew."

"That's the one." Aunt Maybelle bobbed her head. "Do you think she dyed her hair, or was that her natural color?"

The back door opened and in came my sister, Gina, all out of breath from cheerleading practice.

Gina got the looks in our family. She has curly auburn hair, long eyelashes, and a complexion with no zits. She also has a perfect bite, according to the dentist.

"Oh, everything looks so yum!" Gina dropped her things in the den and hurried back to the kitchen. Daphne poured tea into Gina's special mug.

The mug says BORN TO CHEER. Dad got it as a joke, but Gina takes cheerleading very seriously. It's all she ever talks about. Mom said it started back when she was a kid and wanted to be a cheerleader for the Little League. I swear, I think Gina's very first words were "Rah, Rah."

All year long she practices new routines and tries to think up new cheers, most of which are so goofy they're embarrassing.

As we sat at the table, Daphne started up one of her teatime discussions. They were actually kind of fun.

"Today's topic is—if you could have one wish to benefit mankind, what would you wish for?" she asked.

"I wish they could fix the hole in the ozone layer," Brenda said promptly.

"I wish there would be an end to world hunger," Aunt Maybelle said, reaching for another Fig Newton.

"I wish people would stop putting other

people down," I said, thinking of my next-door neighbors, Vonna and Bart.

"And I wish everyone would make an effort to stop pollution," Daphne said.

We looked at Gina, sitting there, deep in thought. Finally she spoke. "I wish I could be head cheerleader next year."

Brenda hooted. "Well, that would certainly benefit mankind."

"Yeah," I chimed in. "It's right up there with world hunger and the ozone layer and pollution. I swear, Gina, sometimes I think your brain is on Call Waiting."

"Oh, that reminds me," Gina said. "Did I get any calls this afternoon?"

You can't even insult Gina. It goes right over her head.

"Yes, you do have a message." Daphne tore a sheet off the pad next to the telephone. "Someone named Bart Peckham called. Is that your boyfriend?"

"Not *Bart* Peckham—you mean *Barf* Peckham." Brenda clutched her throat and gagged. That's the one thing Brenda and I agree on. We can't *stand* Bart Peckham.

"Oh, Bart is just a friend," Gina said. "We hang out with the same crowd. He probably wants to know if I need a ride to the party tonight. Daphne, you did remember to wash my black jeans, didn't you? I want to wear them tonight."

"Not to worry," Daphne reassured her. "I didn't get around to it until this afternoon. But yes, I did wash your jeans and they're in the dryer this very minute."

"*In the dryer?* Oh, no!" Gina cried. "You're *never* supposed to put those jeans in the dryer. They'll shrink right up."

"Oh, dear. I didn't know. I'm terribly sorry," Daphne apologized.

Gina jumped up and rushed to the laundry room. A few seconds later, she returned clutching a pair of jeans that looked as if they belonged to a midget with anorexia.

"Look what you've done! My favorite jeans," she wailed. "What am I supposed to wear tonight?"

I rushed to Daphne's defense. "Stop whining, Gina. You've got plenty of other things to wear."

"But these were my favorite—" Gina started to say when Aunt Maybelle let out a shriek.

"Look at the time! We've already missed five minutes of *Oprah.* Come on, Daphne." Aunt Maybelle steered the housekeeper out of the kitchen.

"Megan, would you be a dear and clean up?" Daphne called over her shoulder.

"Oh, all right," I muttered. Brenda had already hurried back upstairs to finish her homework.

Gina stood there watching me, her eyes wide.

"Does Daphne really expect *you* to clean up?" she asked.

"Housework builds character," I said. "I don't mind housework."

The truth is, I absolutely *hate* housework. But what could I do? A deal is a deal. If I didn't help Daphne around the house, I wouldn't get acting lessons.

Gina lowered her voice. "Daphne is a terrible housekeeper. There's so much dust in the living room, I can write my name on the coffee table."

"Oh, really? You can actually write your name?" I shot back.

As usual, Gina didn't get the sarcasm. "Well, I'm going to tell Mommy and Daddy about this," she huffed. "First Daphne ruins my favorite jeans, and now she's got you doing her work. I hope they get rid of her."

I whirled around. "Listen, Gina," I hissed. "If you say even one word about Daphne, you'll be sorry. I'll tell on you—I mean it. I know all about you."

I didn't know anything at all, but Gina didn't have a clue. "What do you know?" she gasped. "Is it about me and Eric? Or is it what happened at Shawn's party?" My sister was looking at me in wonder, like I had broken some top-secret enemy code. "How did you find out?"

"I have my ways," I said, sounding very mysterious.

"Oh, please, Megan," she begged. "Please don't tell on me. I promise not to say anything about Daphne. I'll even help you clean up."

"Forget it—I'm almost done anyhow." Gina was so useless in the kitchen, she made Daphne look like Wonder Woman.

Gina kept staring at me, shaking her head. "I just can't figure you out. I mean, you've always tried to get rid of all the other housekeepers. But now you're doing everything to make sure Daphne stays here. How come?"

"Because," I said between clenched teeth, "I have seen the light. I realize now how cruel and heartless I've been."

Gina wasn't convinced. "I don't know," she said doubtfully. "You've been acting weird lately, Megan. All that humming you do. And the way you've been so nice to Daphne, helping her and all. Something funny is going on."

"One can change one's mind," I snapped. "It's a sign of maturity."

But, of course, Gina was right. Lately I *was* doing everything possible to make sure Daphne stayed on. I didn't complain when she put garlic powder on the bacon-and-tomato sandwiches. I didn't say a word when she accidentally scorched my favorite blouse. I didn't snitch on her when she knocked over my bedroom lamp and broke it. In fact, I told Mom it was my fault.

It was all so humiliating! How Ella Tinkham and Mavis Feeney and all the other housekeepers I'd gotten rid of would hoot and howl to see me clearing the table and loading the dishwasher and taking out the garbage.

But I didn't have any choice.

I would do *anything* to get the lead in the play!

Chapter 4

"Try it once more, Megan. Legs back against the edge of the chair. Now, ease yourself down gracefully."

"Give me a break, Daphne. I've already done this six times," I whined.

It was Saturday and I was having my acting lesson. Luckily everyone else in the family was out of the house.

Daphne was dressing differently lately. At first she had worn these ridiculous outfits, which she promptly ruined doing housecleaning. She had spilled Clorox on her black velvet pants, ripped the fringe off her cashmere shawl, and accidentally vacuumed one of the buckles off her patent-leather shoes.

That's when she decided maybe a uniform would be more comfortable, so she went out and bought a pink polyester pantsuit. "What do you think?" she'd asked.

"What do I think? I think you look like Aldora Hicks," I'd told her bluntly. "All you need is some pink sponge curlers in your hair."

Daphne tended to dress as if she were playing a role. Today she had on a plain wool skirt and blouse with a gray cardigan over her shoulders, and low-heeled walking shoes. Her hair was pulled back in a neat bun. She looked like she was playing the housekeeper in one of those English mysteries she and Aunt Maybelle always watch on TV.

"An actress has to know how to sit correctly," she said patiently. "By the time we're through, you'll know how to sit and stand and walk—even how to faint onstage."

"How to faint? Aww-*right!*" I said. "At least that'll come in handy. I could pretend to faint at school one of these days and scare everyone."

Daphne smiled. "Oh, Megan, you're too much. Come now, let's give it another try. This time, don't plop down."

She made me practice sitting down gracefully three more times until I got it right.

"You're doing fine," Daphne told me. "And I can tell you've been practicing the breathing exercises. It makes such a difference in your voice. However," she said, giving my shoulders a thump, "we need to work on your posture."

Before I knew what was happening, Daphne

took one of Aunt Maybelle's romance novels from the coffee table and handed it to me. "I want you to practice walking around with this book on your head."

"This sucker is heavy," I complained. "It feels like a lead weight."

"Well, if you want to play the part of a princess, you have to carry yourself like one," Daphne reminded me.

"Oh, all right." I felt like a fool, walking around with *So Wild the Passion* wobbling on my head.

"That's how you develop poise and good posture," Daphne told me cheerfully. "Now let's go into the kitchen. Careful! Keep the book on your—*oops!*"

The book kept falling off until I got the hang of balancing it on my head.

"The real trick is to be able to go about your business without dropping the book," Daphne said as she started clearing the lunch dishes. "Do you think you could help me clean up and still keep the book on your head?"

"Sure I can." To prove it, I wiped the table and rinsed the dishes. I was about to put them in the dishwasher when Jeremy came in unexpectedly. I was so surprised I nearly dropped the book.

"Don't scare me like that, Jeremy. I could

have broken my toe if this fell on me."

He stood there gawking. *"Now* what are you up to? How come you've got that big book on your head?"

I let Daphne explain. "Megan is learning to walk with poise and grace," she told Jeremy. "Now Megan is going to see if she can take out the garbage and still keep the book balanced on her head."

"Bet she can't," Jeremy snorted.

"Bet I can," I snapped.

Daphne placed the book back on my head and handed me a brown paper bag that felt soggy at the bottom. She opened the back door and I walked down the steps carefully.

"You're doing fine," Daphne said. "Just one more step."

I took the last step carefully to show Jeremy how graceful and poised I was.

"What the heck!" cried a loud voice.

I was so startled, I jumped. The book fell off my head and into the garbage bag, which promptly split open. Once again Daphne had broken the garbage disposal, so the bag was full of coffee grounds, eggshells, soggy bread crusts, and other gross things, which now spilled out all over the ground.

For a moment I didn't realize who had sneaked up on me. Then I recognized that stupid laugh. Who else could it be but Bart Peckham, Vonna Mae's brother.

"Look what you made me do!" I sputtered.

Daphne and Jeremy rushed out to help pick up the garbage.

"Where's Gina?" Bart wanted to know.

"She's at her friend's house," Daphne told him.

"Oh. I thought maybe she felt like going for a ride or something." Bart stood there, hands in his pockets, watching us pick up garbage and not even offering to help.

"Hey, Megan," he said, jutting his receding chin in my direction, "what were you doing with that book on your head? Getting ready for a beauty contest?"

Before I could answer, Jeremy said, "She's getting ready for tryouts. She's sure to beat out your sister."

"Tryouts? You mean tryouts for the school play?" Bart said. "Vonna is trying out for the lead."

"Well, so is Megan," Jeremy told him.

I wish Jeremy would learn to keep his mouth shut.

"Megan?" Bart started to laugh. "That's a joke."

Daphne stared at him coldly. "Why, may I ask, is that such a joke?"

"Are you kidding? Megan, an actress? She couldn't act her way out of a paper bag. Unless," he snickered, "she was playing the part of a brat—you know, just playing herself."

Bart was still laughing as he headed back to his house, cutting through the hedge that separates our yards.

"Megan happens to be a very good actress," Daphne called after him.

"That guy is a slime bucket," Jeremy said. He looked at me and said quietly, "I'm sorry I mentioned the play, Megan. It just slipped out."

As he walked back into the house, Daphne said, "Megan, please don't let someone like Bart upset you. He's a fool. It's not worth getting mad at him."

"I don't get mad," I told Daphne. "I get *even!*"

Later, Daphne went upstairs to take her usual Saturday afternoon nap. Jeremy and I sat around in the den, trying to think of something fun to do.

Jeremy happened to be looking out the window at the Peckham house when he suddenly burst out laughing.

"Quick—you've got to check out the scene next door. Bart is standing in front of the window with his shirt off, lifting weights."

"Spare me," I said. "My heart can't take such excitement."

We watched Bart for a few minutes. "I didn't know Barfy was into bodybuilding," Jeremy said.

"He ought to be into *brain*-building," I retorted. "What a show-off. Look how he's posing there, right in front of the window."

"Maybe he thinks he'll give Gina and her friends a thrill." Jeremy snickered. "What a conceited jerk he is."

That's when the brilliant Get Even Plan hit me!

So Bart didn't think I could act? Well, I'd show *him* what a good actress I was!

"Quick, Jer, close the blinds. I'm going upstairs to play a telephone trick."

Bart answered the phone on the fifth ring. "Bart Peckham here," he said smartly, Mister Cool himself. It was all I could do not to burst out laughing.

I took a deep breath, the way Daphne had taught me, so my voice would be in a lower range. Those exercises really do make a difference.

"You don't know me, Bart," I said in my vibrant new voice. "But I happened to see you around, and I found out your name. I think you're really cute."

"Oh, yeah?" Bart was cautious. "Where'd you see me?"

"Uh, I think you were . . . washing your car." I figured that was a pretty smart answer. Bart is always washing his car. It's probably the hardest work he ever does. I don't think he washes *himself* that often.

"Anyhow," I went on, "I found out your name, like I said. I hope you don't think I'm *pushy,* calling you and all."

"That's okay," Bart said generously. "Lots of girls do."

Yeah, right. In your dreams, Barfy.

I knew how he loved flattery. "You look like you work out a lot," I said. "Are you into body-building and stuff?"

That seemed to break the ice. "I lift weights. Matter of fact, that's what I was doing when the phone rang." Bart started to talk so much about lifting weights that I thought I'd fall asleep.

Meanwhile, I could hear Jeremy's loud breathing on the extension downstairs. He has all kinds of allergies, and sometimes his breathing sounds like a hornet's nest.

"Hey," Bart said suddenly, "what's that funny noise? Is someone listening on your phone?"

I had to think fast. "No, we've got this new cordless phone and there's a lot of static on it."

"Yeah, that happens on ours, too," Bart said. "So, what else do you want to know about me? I'm six feet tall . . ."

Six feet tall? I bit my cheek so I wouldn't laugh. Bart wouldn't be six feet tall if they stretched him on a rack for a year.

". . . and I've got good muscles," he bragged.

Good muscles? I've seen better muscles on a Perdue chicken!

Bart was getting carried away as he went on and on about how terrific he was. Finally he said, "Hey, by the way, what's *your* name?"

I drew a blank. I couldn't think of a good name to use. Allison? Brittany? Samantha? I glanced frantically around the room and finally spotted one of the books Brenda had taken out of the library for a book report. It was *National Velvet*.

"Um, my name is Velvet," I gulped.

"Velvet," Bart repeated slowly. "Wow. I never knew anybody with a name like that. Your voice is like velvet too, ya know?"

Suddenly, he was very interested in me. Where did I live? How old was I? Where did I go to school? How come he never heard of me?

My mind was racing. "We just moved here. Well, actually I don't live in Winslow exactly. I live in one of the towns nearby." I told him I was seventeen and went to a private girls' school, but I couldn't give him my telephone number because my parents were very, very strict.

"Yeah, but what do you *look* like?" Bart

wanted to know. "I mean, are you good-looking? A dog? Or what?"

I couldn't believe anyone would ask such a dumb question. But then again, Bart Peckham is *not* the brightest bulb in the circuit.

"Well, Bart, I don't want to sound *conceited—*" I gave a throaty laugh "—but, well, everyone says I'm gorgeous. I have long blond hair and emerald eyes."

"Emerald? That's uh . . ."

"That's *green*." Bart was so dumb I couldn't believe it. "Also, I've got a great body, if I do say so myself. I'm planning to be a model."

"That good?" Bart was impressed. "Say, listen, Velvet, when can we get together?"

I was about to reply when I heard Jeremy put down the phone and rush upstairs. "Hold on a sec," I said.

Jeremy was waving furiously. "Gina and her friend are coming up the walk," he whispered.

"Who's that talking to you?" Bart demanded.

"It's my kid brother. He says my dad needs to use the phone. I have to go now."

"Hey, wait, Velvet. I don't have your phone number. How can I get in touch with you?"

"I'll try to call you sometime. Bye-bye." I blew a loud kiss into the phone and hung up.

Just in time. Gina and her friend, Tiffany, came into the room, looking very excited.

"Megan, Jeremy, we want to show you our new cheer. I thought it up myself," Gina said proudly.

"Oh, all right, but you better be careful," I warned her. "No cartwheels or somersaults. Last time you did one of your routines, you broke a lamp. Let's go into the den."

Downstairs, Gina and Tiffany stood in the middle of the room, looking solemn. They sure take their cheerleading responsibilities seriously.

They clapped and kicked and did little steps as they chanted:

Winslow High, you're the best.
You stand out from all the rest.
Look to the east, look to the west.
Winslow High, you're the best!

At the end they did a high jump and the furniture shook. Luckily, nothing broke.

"Well, what do you think?" Gina's cheeks were pink with excitement. "I thought up that cheer all by myself."

"Sure gave *me* goosebumps," I said with a perfectly straight face.

"Really?" Gina said happily. "Me, too!"

There was a loud pounding at the back door. It was none other than Bart Peckham, out of breath, buttoning up his shirt. He must have run like a rabbit to our house.

"Saw your car in the driveway, Gina . . ." *Huff-puff.* "Wanted to tell you . . ." *Huff-puff.* "Won't believe it . . ."

"Won't believe *what?"* Tiffany batted her pale yellow eyelashes at him. She's always had a thing for Bart. I guess there's no accounting for weird taste.

"It finally happened . . ." *Huff-puff.* "Old Cupid got Bart Peckham right *here!"*

Bart pointed to where his heart was supposed to be.

"What are you talking about?" Gina asked.

Finally Bart caught his breath. "Okay. There's this great-looking chick who just moved here. She saw me washing my car one day." He paused for effect. "The rest is history."

Tiffany's eyes narrowed. "A new girl? I haven't heard about anyone new moving here. What's her name?"

"Well, she doesn't live in Winslow. She lives in one of the other towns." Bart gestured vaguely. "I think maybe she said Farmington. Anyhow, she goes to a private school."

He grabbed Tiffany and whirled her around the kitchen as if they were ballroom dancing.

"I am in L-O-V-E!" he sang at the top of his lungs.

"Who says Bart Peckham can't spell?" I remarked.

"What did you say this girl's name was?" Tiffany asked.

"Her name," Bart said reverently, "is *Velvet."*

Jeremy caught my eye, and the two of us crept quietly out of the kitchen. We had to clamp our hands over our mouths to keep from laughing out loud as we ran downstairs to the basement, where nobody could hear us.

"Uh-oh," Jeremy said when we finally caught our breath. "Look what you've started, Megan. What are you going to do *now?"*

Chapter 5

"Everything looks great, hon." Dad beamed at Mom. "It seems like a long time since the whole family had dinner together."

It was Wednesday, Daphne's day off, and she was out for the evening. Wonder of wonders, Mom had gotten home early for a change. She'd even cooked dinner instead of bringing home pizza or something from the deli.

In fact, she had fixed my favorite—teriyaki roast beef with mushrooms, onions, and roast potatoes.

Aunt Maybelle took a big second helping. "Delicious, Anne," she said with her mouth full.

"Oh, Mummy, this is yummy!" Gina said. Gina makes everything sound like a cheer.

"Flattery will get you everywhere," Mom said with a smile as she brought the marinated green beans to the table.

It was nice having Mom around, just like old

times. When Mom isn't tired or busy, she's a lot of fun. She's always laughing and joking.

She's put on weight since she started Let Mama Do It. You'd think with all that running around, she'd lose weight. But she says it's because she's always on the go and doesn't eat right. Mom's also been too busy to go to the hairdresser. Instead, she pulls her hair back in an old-fashioned bun. There's lots more gray in it, too. Dad doesn't seem to mind. He says she looks more like a mama that way.

Dinner was fun. Dad was teasing Mom about being a local celebrity. "The *Winslow Dispatch* is doing a feature story on your mother," he told us proudly. "And next month she's giving a talk at the Jaycees meeting."

My parents are the only married people I know who really seem to like each other. It's too bad they're both so busy and we don't see much of them.

The telephone interrupted dinner. Mom's clients are always interrupting dinner, even though she's asked them not to call in the evening unless it's an emergency.

"That was Mr. Fenster," Mom said apologetically as she hurried back to the table. "He's checking to be sure his manuscript is safe."

We all groaned. Mom has some wacky clients, but J. Ogden Fenster could win the

Looney Tunes Lifetime Achievement Award. Whenever he calls he refers to himself as "J. Ogden Fenster, Author." Actually, he's never had anything published, even though he says he's written six books.

Mr. Fenster is convinced that editors want to steal his ideas, so he won't send out his manuscripts to any publishing houses.

Not that anyone would ever want to publish his books. I tried to read his stuff once, and I nearly fell asleep. It's so dull—he writes such long sentences and nothing ever happens.

Anyhow, Mr. Fenster had Mom type up his most recent manuscript, then insisted that she keep it locked up at our house. He was worried that someone might break into his apartment and steal his literary treasure.

The telephone rang once more. Dad jumped up to answer it. "Good news," he reported when he came back to the table. "Mr. Fenster is stopping by later to pick up his manuscript. He's decided to keep it in his safe-deposit box."

"Thank goodness," Mom said. "I'm tired of having him call me at all hours to make sure it hasn't been stolen."

I giggled. "Who'd want to steal it anyhow? J. Ogden Fenster could only sell that book to people with insomnia. It would put them right to sleep."

Everyone laughed. We were relieved to be rid of both J. O. Fenster, author, and his Great American Novel—at least until he wrote another book.

"So, what's new with everyone?" Mom wanted to know. "I need to catch up on things."

Aunt Maybelle had a major news bulletin. After years of faithfully watching television from morning to night, a ratings survey had finally called her and asked what shows she watched.

"It was a nice, long interview," Aunt Maybelle reported happily. "The lady said my comments were very valuable."

"Oh, Auntie, that's wonderful," Mom said. "It's about time they called you."

Gina had something to contribute. "Greg Walsh asked me to his senior prom."

Everyone was duly impressed because Greg Walsh is the jock of Winslow High.

After Gina and Mom discussed what kind of prom dress to buy, Mom turned to me. "How about you, Megan? What's happening with you these days?"

I racked my brain for something to say. Should I tell them that I was stringing Bart Peckham along, pretending to be Velvet, the girl with the emerald eyes?

Or should I tell them how I phoned Mrs. Peckham and pretended I was conducting a survey. I had asked Mrs. Peckham what size bra she wore, and she'd actually told me!

Or maybe I should tell them how I made an old lady happy. I had phoned Aunt Maybelle from Jeremy's house, saying I was from the television rating service and would she mind answering some questions.

Finally I decided that just about everything I'd done lately would probably get me in trouble, so it was smarter to just keep my mouth shut.

"Nothing much is new," I replied with a shrug.

Mom looked at Brenda, who was sitting there absently eating with one hand and holding her science book with the other. "I heard you got an A on your science project, Brenda."

My sister didn't answer. She kept on reading. That always bugs me. I keep telling my parents it's bad manners for someone to sit and read at the dinner table. But they figure Brenda is so brilliant they don't want to stop her quest for knowledge—not even to pass the potatoes.

"It's extremely rude of Brenda to just sit there with her nose in a book," I reminded my parents.

Mom sighed. "Well, Amy Carter always used to read at the dinner table when her father was in the White House."

"Who's Amy Carter?" Gina wanted to know.

"She's the daughter of former president Jimmy Carter," Dad said.

Aunt Maybelle looked up from her plate. "I always wondered—were those Jimmy Carter's own teeth?"

The conversation was going off on a tangent, the way it often did with Aunt Maybelle. Brenda just sat there, reading her book. I *know* she hears everything, even if she pretends not to.

I wasn't finished discussing Brenda. "Daphne says it's bad manners, too. She won't allow Brenda to read at the table when we have afternoon tea."

"Oh, I wish Daphne was home to watch *Jeopardy* with me tonight," Aunt Maybelle said. "She's so good at it. She knows all the answers."

"Sure." Gina snickered. "That's because Daphne's always parked in front of the TV set instead of—"

I shot Gina a look and she said quickly, "What I mean is, I guess Daphne learned a lot from television."

"That reminds me, where *is* Daphne tonight?" Dad asked. "Where does she go on Wednesdays?"

"She does some kind of volunteer work," Mom said. "She told me what it was, but I forgot."

I looked up in surprise. "I didn't know Daphne did any volunteer work," I said.

"Daphne is a lady of mystery," Dad said.

"The real mystery is, what does she *do* all day?" Mom laughed. "She certainly isn't going to win the Good Housekeeping Award."

"Daphne really does try," Aunt Maybelle put in.

I gave Gina a poke in the ribs. "Uh . . . Daphne is . . . um . . . very good," she said.

Brenda suddenly came to life. She put down her book and said, "Daphne helped me with my science project."

My father looked impressed. "Well, I see Daphne has some loyal fans. However, we haven't heard from the toughest critic of them all." He gave me a wink. "Well, Megan, what do *you* think of Daphne?"

I nearly choked. Was I actually going to have to say something *nice* about a housekeeper? "She's okay," I mumbled.

Mom gave me a funny look. "You and Daphne have really hit it off, haven't you? You seem to have a lot to talk about with each other." Was it my imagination, or did Mom sound a little bit jealous?

"Is Daphne's cooking getting any better?" Dad asked. "I haven't been home that much lately."

"It's pretty good," I answered, choosing my words carefully. "I mean, nothing compares to *Mom's* cooking . . ."

Dad clapped loudly and Mom wagged her finger at me. "Oh, no, you don't. I know what you guys are up to. You're trying to put me on a guilt trip, aren't you?"

Ever since my mother got involved in that business of hers, she's been talking about guilt trips. She says we make her feel guilty because she doesn't cook as much as she used to and she's usually with her clients when we really need her at home.

As a joke Dad had a special T-shirt made for her that said, IF IT WEREN'T FOR GUILT TRIPS, I'D *NEVER* GO ON VACATION.

Over dessert my parents started discussing things that needed to be done around the house. "Don't forget," I reminded them, "you promised to fix up the attic so I can have my own room again."

Mom and Dad planned to have an extra room made in the attic for me. That would be great. I was hoping to get my own telephone and have some privacy, especially for my telephone tricks.

"We're planning on having the work done this summer," Dad said. "But it's going to be pretty expensive."

"Not as expensive as sending me to a psychiatrist," I said. "Brenda is driving me crazy."

Mom laughed. "Oh, come on, Megan. How

could Brenda bother anyone? She's so quiet and studious."

"Are you kidding?" I've tried to tell Mom how awful it's been sharing a room with Brenda, but Mom just doesn't seem to listen to me lately.

Just then Brenda put down her book. I thought she was about to start arguing with me, but instead she announced, "Miss Brennan says I have the highest average in the class."

Everyone made a big fuss over that.

Not to be outdone, Gina spoke up. "Everyone thinks I'll make head cheerleader next year."

That got a good amount of attention, too.

As usual, I didn't have anything to contribute. I wanted to brag a little, too. Except I didn't have anything to brag about.

A familiar empty feeling came over me. It reminded me of the time, a few years ago, when Uncle Jack was introducing us to his new wife.

"This is the beauty." He pointed to Gina. "This is the brain." He patted Brenda's head. "And this," he said, pinching my cheek, "is the brat."

That really hurt my feelings. Up till then Uncle Jack had been my favorite relative. Maybe he didn't really mean it, but it bothered me.

Suddenly, I couldn't help blurting out, "I may have some big news, too, pretty soon."

Of course, everyone wanted to know what my big news was.

"It's a surprise," I said. "Only Daphne knows what it is." I figured that would explain why I was in Daphne's company so much.

"You won't even tell *me,* Megan?" Mom sounded hurt and I felt glad.

My sisters kept pestering me, wanting to know what my surprise was. But of course I wouldn't tell them.

I wouldn't tell anyone until tryouts were over and I could brag, too—about getting the part of Princess Leyla in the play.

It was all I could do not to shout, "Move over, gorgeous Gina and brilliant Brenda. Make way for marvelous Megan!"

Chapter 6

On the way home from school the next day, I overheard Vonna bragging that she was going to have her hair cut and styled at an expensive beauty salon in Boston.

"It costs a fortune," she told Saralee. "But my mother says I'm worth it. She wants me to look extra pretty for tryouts."

That's when I started getting nervous.

I mean, I'd never given a thought about how my hair should look, tryouts or otherwise. I just wash it, rub it with a towel, and let it dry any old way.

But after hearing what Vonna said, I realized I would need to look as good as possible for tryouts. And they were only a week away.

Jeremy said I should ask Daphne to help me with my hair. We cornered her as soon as we got home.

Daphne examined me critically. "Your hair

would look much better if you blew it dry. Why don't you wet down your hair and I'll see what I can do."

Jeremy watched as Daphne glopped on mousse and gel. Then she spritzed and sprayed and whirled and twirled the hairbrush.

When she was through, Jeremy said, "Hey, that looks good."

I had to admit my hair *did* look nicer. "But it's too much work," I complained. "I'm only going to fix it like this the day of tryouts."

Daphne didn't stop with my hair. She tweezed my eyebrows, too, and gave me a manicure.

Then, after Jeremy went home, she dragged me upstairs to look through my closet and pick out an outfit to wear for tryouts.

I refused to wear a skirt. We finally settled on gray slacks and a pink blouse.

The next day at lunch, Vonna announced she was also having a facial at that beauty salon.

"A facial cleans your pores," she explained to Saralee. "And it's supposed to make your skin glow."

I sighed. Was this ever going to stop? I glanced at myself in the girls' room mirror and decided I ought to do something about my skin, too. It was pale and blah-looking and didn't glow at all. My pores probably needed cleaning, too.

That evening, I went into Gina's room and sneaked out her Purifying Vitamin E Miracle Facial Mask. I locked myself in the bathroom while the mask was hardening so nobody could see what I was doing.

It felt like I had glue on my face. I sure was glad when I finally washed off that sticky mask.

So where was the vibrant glow I was supposed to get? If anything, my face looked paler than ever!

As long as I had the bathroom to myself, I decided to practice my voice exercises. I ran the water loud, so nobody could hear me. *"Guns and drums,"* I chanted. *"Drums and guns."*

I'd had to cut down on my humming because Brenda heard me and complained that I sounded like a bumblebee.

Glancing at myself in the mirror once more, I noticed there were dark circles under my eyes. What I needed most of all, I decided, was a good night's sleep.

I padded back to my room to get ready for bed. Actually, I don't know why I even call it *my* room. It's not my room anymore—not since Brilliant Brenda moved in.

She was sitting up in bed, reading a history book. Except for the fact that she's skinny and wears glasses, Brenda looked a lot like me—brown eyes, straight brown hair, very ordinary.

"Did you set the alarm?" she asked, not even glancing up from her book.

"How come you always ask me that?" I kicked off my slippers and hopped into bed. "You ask me that same dumb question every single night."

I pulled the blanket over my head. But tired as I was, I couldn't sleep. I kept thinking about tryouts next week, and all kinds of crazy thoughts started going through my head.

Suppose I get stage fright? Suppose I trip and fall? Suppose I have to go to the bathroom really bad in the middle of tryouts? Suppose—

It was no use. I just couldn't sleep. I sat up and looked at Brenda. I must have been really desperate for conversation because I said, "Hey, want to talk? We hardly ever talk to each other."

She gave me a suspicious look. "What do you want to talk about?"

"I don't know. We could talk about Mom's business. Doesn't it bother you that she's hardly ever—"

"No, let's talk about Ella Tinkham," Brenda cut in. "Tell me how you got rid of her. I was busy doing a science project when she left, and I always wondered what happened."

"Oh, all right." I leaned back against the pillow and told Brenda the story.

Of all the housekeepers Mom hired, Ella Tinkham was the meanest. She was big and red-faced, and she ordered us around like an army sergeant, which, we found out, she used to be.

Nothing scared Ella Tinkham. Well, almost nothing.

"Except snakes," she confided, her little eyes narrowing. "I hate them slimy things."

That gave me an idea. I remembered that Jeremy's father had bought a black rubber snake to keep pigeons away from their patio. I borrowed the rubber snake and put it in Ella's underwear drawer.

She let out a yell you could have heard in Outer Mongolia.

My parents raced upstairs to see what all the commotion was about. They checked every drawer in the dresser, they went through the closet, they even moved all the furniture.

Meanwhile, of course, I had taken the rubber snake out of the drawer.

"I *know* that creepy thing is crawling around this house somewhere," Ella had declared. "I won't sleep a wink."

The next night, when Ella went to brush her dentures, there was a black snake coiled outside the bathroom. *"There it is again!"* she hollered.

Dad picked up the snake and gave her a strange look. "Ella, this is Gina's black leather belt."

From then on, things went downhill. Ella

shrieked when she spotted a length of coiled clothesline in the back yard. She screamed when she saw what looked like a garter snake on my bed.

"But Ella," I said innocently, "it's only the green belt from my bathrobe."

The next day Ella packed her suitcases and informed us she was going to live with her sister in Minnesota, where it was cold but at least there weren't many snakes.

When I finished the story, Brenda said, "Oh, so that's what happened."

The she wiped her glasses on the pillowcase, put them on, and started reading her history book again.

So much for trying to have a normal conversation with Brenda.

I pulled the blanket over my head so the light wouldn't bother me. I was just starting to doze off when she began making those disgusting noises of hers.

When Brenda is concentrating on her homework, she clicks her tongue and makes slurping sounds.

I tried to ignore them. But then she started to flip the pages of her book. You wouldn't believe how *loud* she flips them.

Flip-flip-flip. Click-click-click. Tch-tch-tch. Slurp-slurp-slurp.

"Knock it off, Brenda," I complained. "If you don't shut off the light and stop making those noises, I'm calling Mom and Dad in here."

"Go ahead," Brenda said spitefully, "and I'll tell them how you got rid of Ella Tinkham."

Do you believe anybody could be so *rotten?*

Finally she shut off the light and fell asleep as soon as her head hit the pillow, while I lay there, tossing and turning.

There was no doubt about it. There was no way I could wait until summer for my parents to fix up the extra room for me.

I was going to lose my marbles sharing my bedroom with Brenda. As soon as tryouts are over, I promised myself, I'll think of a way to get rid of Daphne.

But then a funny feeling gnawed at my conscience. Daphne had been really nice to me. Maybe she can stay on with us for a while, I thought. I can probably put up with Brenda for another few months. . . .

At that moment, Brenda turned over and started to make slurping noises in her sleep.

That did it!

It's either bye-bye, Daphne or hello, funny farm, I decided.

That was my last thought before I finally drifted off to sleep.

Chapter 7

Daphne sat on the sofa, pencil poised over her notebook so she could write down comments. "Give it a try, Megan."

"I feel so dumb," I told her.

It was Saturday afternoon and everyone was out of the house. Daphne said Saturday was the best time to work on the more challenging acting projects.

Like this one.

"You need to be aware of all the inflections in your voice," Daphne explained. "So I want you to say, 'Oh, John' twenty different ways."

Acting was not as easy as I had thought. "There's no way you can say 'Oh, John' twenty different ways," I protested.

"Yes, you can. Here's one way." Daphne made her shoulders droop, and said in a sorrowful voice, "Oh, John."

Then she changed expression and her voice

rose in a cry of warning. *"Oh, John!"*

She smiled. "You see? Those are two very different inflections. There are so many ways to say 'Oh, John' . . . with anger, concern, reproach. Try it."

"All right, all right," I grumbled. I sucked in my stomach, pulled back my shoulders, and flared my nostrils to get in the mood.

"Oh, John," I said with a sneer.

"Good, Megan. Now another."

This time I said, "Oh, John" in a tone of regret. Then I said it in a tone of amazement. Then in anger.

To my surprise, I was able to come up with fifteen different-sounding "Oh, Johns."

Daphne cheered me on. "Keep going. Think of the different shadings. Think of romance. Think of this person named John. Try to visualize him."

I tried to visualize someone named John. But all I could picture was John Jacintho, who's the shortest kid in my class. It was hard to think of him romantically.

Then I got an idea. I thought about Randy Howard.

And I didn't even realize I was saying "Oh, John" in a teasing, playful voice.

And then in a romantic voice, as if I were Princess Leyla, "Oh, John."

I didn't quite make it to twenty, but Daphne said I did very well for someone my age.

That made me feel so good that I decided to call up Bart Peckham and practice my inflections on him. When Daphne went upstairs to finish straightening the bedrooms, I raced to the telephone.

Bart was thrilled to hear from me.

"Velvet, where have you been? You haven't called me in a long time."

"I called you a few days ago," I reminded him.

"Yeah, but it seems longer than that."

"Well," I told him, "I've been busy."

"Oh, yeah? What *kind* of busy?" he demanded.

"This and that," I said.

"Were you . . ." He paused, then blurted out, "Were you *boyfriend* busy? Are you going with someone?"

"Why, Bart, I do believe you're jealous." I gave a tinkly laugh and without thinking used one of those twenty different inflections. "Oh, John!" I said.

"John!" He choked. "Who's *John?* I'm Bart, remember?"

Quickly I corrected myself. "I meant to say, 'Oh, Bart.' "

"Yeah? Well, who's this guy *John*?"

"John is . . . uh . . . my kid brother. You remember, the pesky kid who always bugs me."

Bart sounded relieved. "Oh. I thought maybe John was your boyfriend."

"My boyfriend? Oh, Bart!" That was the warm, romantic inflection.

There was a silence on the other end. "What's the matter?" I asked.

"It's the way you say my name. Your voice really gets to me." Bart cleared his throat. "Velvet, when am I gonna get to meet you?"

"One of these days, I promise."

"I told my friends all about you. They want to meet you, too."

"Oh, don't worry," I said sweetly. "They'll get to meet me."

"Yeah, but when?" Bart asked. "And where?"

I heard Daphne coming down the stairs. "I'll think of something," I said quickly. Then I hung up the telephone just as she came into the room.

The rest of the afternoon was long and dreary. Maybe that was because it was raining. Or maybe it was because Jeremy wasn't around. He had gone with his parents to New Hampshire for the weekend.

Everyone in my family was busy with something. Everyone except me, of course. My parents were going to a play in Boston. Gina was going to a Sweet Sixteen Party. Aunt Maybelle was going line dancing at the Senior Center. And Brenda was doing a project for extra credit.

Even Daphne was busy, writing letters in her bedroom.

I was so bored that I actually did my homework, even though it was only Saturday and I usually leave everything till Sunday night. We had to write a character description for the Creative Writing Workshop at school.

I wrote a description of Aunt Maybelle about to start on another one of her diets. Then I decided I didn't want anyone to recognize her in case Mrs. Caron read the papers aloud in class. So I disguised Aunt Maybelle's appearance. I gave her red hair and made her thirty years younger and forty pounds lighter.

When that was finished, I did my math. I was thinking about sneaking in a quick call to Wilfred Boggs when Daphne came downstairs and announced she wanted to take Brenda and me out for pizza.

"My treat," she said. "I think we need a break on such a dreary night, don't you?"

Much as I wanted pizza, I felt guilty about having Daphne treat us. I didn't want her being so nice, because then I'd feel bad when I had to get rid of her after tryouts.

We arrived at Pizza Heaven before the crowd, so we were able to get the back booth.

It's my favorite spot because I can see everyone from there, but they can't see me.

"Mmmmm." Daphne gave an appreciative sniff. "It smells wonderful. I can see why everyone in town comes here."

She and I ordered pizza with pepperoni and mushrooms.

Brenda, being the pill she is, didn't want pizza. Instead, she ordered spaghetti with marinara sauce. As soon as the waitress brought it over, Brenda began to cut up the spaghetti into little pieces. The marinara sauce splattered all over me.

"Look what you did! This is my favorite blouse," I complained as I dabbed at the stain with a wet napkin. "You are such a slob, Brenda."

"Oh, stuff it," she said. "In fact, stuff it sideways."

"You might get all A's in school," I snapped, "but you are definitely lacking in the social graces."

With that, I took a bite of pizza and burned the roof of my mouth. It was torture, but I wouldn't even say ouch because I didn't want to give my sister the satisfaction.

Brenda finished dissecting her spaghetti. Then she looked at Daphne and said, "So where do you go on Wednesday nights anyhow?"

One thing about Brenda: She gets right to the point.

"You are such a jerk," I told her. "I liked it better when you had your nose in a book."

"And *I'd* like it better if you had your nose in a meat grinder," she shot back.

Daphne started to laugh. "The two of you sound like my sister and me when we were your age. All right, Brenda, in answer to your question, on Wednesday nights, I'm a reader with the Guild for the Blind. I make recordings of local news items and the library sends them out on cassettes to blind people. I've been a volunteer reader for years, wherever I've lived."

"Oh." Brenda sounded disappointed, as if she were hoping that maybe Daphne was a cat burglar who robbed rich people every Wednesday night. "Does that have anything to do with that decision you have to make?"

"No," Daphne replied. She was quiet for a moment. Finally she heaved a sigh and said, "I have to decide whether I want to get married or continue my acting career."

Daphne had told me about her boyfriend, Edgar Kimball. She had met him four years ago when she was doing summer stock on Cape Cod. Edgar owned a hardware store in Swansea, a small town about an hour and a half away from Winslow. He was a widower with two children, he had a lovely house, and he was sweet, kind, patient, and wonderful.

"I have to make up my mind once and for all." Daphne pushed her plate away. "It's either Edgar or the theater."

"Why can't you have both?" I put in. "If Edgar is so terrific, why don't you marry him and keep on with your acting."

Daphne's eyes grew misty. "Oh, Edgar is very understanding. He'd love for me to keep on with my career. But it's not that simple. He owns a business and he has two kids, so naturally he doesn't want to move. If we got married, I'd have to live in Swansea. It's such a small town and there are really no theater opportunities there."

"What I don't understand," said Brenda, "is why you decided to come to Winslow and be a housekeeper."

"I suppose it does sound strange, but I honestly didn't know what else to do," Daphne explained. "I felt I just had to get away from everyone and everything. I needed to think things out. I wanted to see what it would be like living in a small town, taking care of a house, being part of a family. And then I remembered driving through Winslow one summer years back and thinking what a pretty town it was. So I came here and registered with the employment agency, and your mother hired me."

The explanation apparently satisfied Brenda because she just nodded, stood up, and went off to the ladies' room without even saying "Excuse me." I've noticed that a lot of people who are very smart have very poor manners.

When Brenda was gone, I asked Daphne what she thought her decision was going to be.

"I'm just as mixed up as ever," she said ruefully. "I had given myself a timetable of three months to make a decision. The three months will be up just about the time of your school play, Megan."

I was stunned. "Hey, wait a minute, Daphne. You mean you were only planning to stay with us for three months and then you were going to leave?"

Daphne nodded. "That's right. I had an agreement with your mother. When she hired me, I told her this would only be a temporary job for me. No matter whether I decide to marry Edgar or move back to New York, I'll be leaving."

I couldn't believe it. All this time I had been thinking about how to get rid of Daphne and feeling guilty about it. Then, tonight when she invited us out for pizza, I had even considered letting her stay on.

And now she had told me that she was only going to be with us a few months! To my surprise, I felt an unexpected sense of loss.

Brenda returned from the ladies' room and the two of us managed to start arguing again. I don't think we used to fight so much before Mom started up her business.

"Come on, you two, lighten up and—" Daphne broke off and started to laugh. "Well, look who just came in."

I glanced at the doorway. Oh, joy of joys. There stood Bart and a couple of his friends.

It's a good thing I had finished eating. Otherwise, I would have lost my appetite listening to Mister Personality as he called out greetings to people he knew.

"Yo, Scott." Bart's voice could be heard over the clatter of dishes. "Yo, Debby. Yo, Jimbo."

"That Bart—he's a regular yo-yo," Brenda remarked, and we all broke up. I didn't realize my sister could be so funny.

Bart and his buddies were seated at a nearby table, so I could hear everything he was talking about. Such as, how the waitress was giving him the eye, how much the new tape deck for his car cost, and how this girl named Velvet was just crazy about him.

"Yeah, she called me up this afternoon," he bragged. "That Velvet—she's got it bad for me . . . Yeah, sure, you'll get to meet her soon . . . Well, like I told you, her parents are very strict, that's why . . ."

I was so busy listening to Barfy that I didn't realize Daphne and Brenda were putting on their raincoats.

"Wake up, little Suzie." Daphne waved her hand in front of my face. "We're ready to leave."

As I got up from the booth, another electrifying idea came to me.

It was the perfect way to get even!

Bart had asked when and where he could meet Velvet. Now I had an answer for him.

When? On Friday evening, May 24th, around 10 P.M.—right after our school play was over.

Where? Right here—at Pizza Heaven!

Chapter 8

Mrs. Caron read the character description aloud and looked around the room. "Are there any comments? Jeremy—no? Beth?"

I slunk down in my seat, hoping Mrs. Caron wouldn't call on me. Sometimes I get carried away when she asks for comments on our creative writing assignments. The paper she had just read was a description of somebody's grandfather.

Vonna and Saralee were whispering to each other, and Mrs. Caron spotted them. "Well, Vonna, apparently you have something to say. Would you please share your comments with the rest of us?"

"Oh, I thought the description was just wonderful," Vonna said, blushing prettily.

"What, specifically, did you find 'wonderful,' Vonna?" Mrs. Caron asked.

"Oh, um, like—" Vonna was flustered. "Well, you know, like, how that old man looked and—"

Mrs. Caron cut her off. "Remember, classroom participation counts in your grade." Her eyes caught mine. "Did anyone notice any trite words, overworked phrases? What about you, Megan?"

"Well," I said slowly, "in the part about the grandfather's hands folded neatly in his lap . . ."

I heard Vonna snicker, but I plunged on. "Well, that phrase doesn't make sense to me. I mean, could you fold your hands *sloppily?"*

Vonna and Saralee were giggling. Mrs. Caron frowned at them and turned to Randy Howard. "Well, Randy, what do you think about Megan's comments? Can you think of another way to describe your grandfather's hands without reference to their being neatly folded?"

Randy just smiled and gave a little shrug.

That was Randy's paper? Oh, no! My face turned red.

He must think I'm a total idiot. First I'd played a telephone trick on him and he'd recognized my voice. And now I'd practically torn apart his Creative Writing assignment.

Just then the bell rang. I jumped up as fast as I could. Behind me, I could hear Vonna gushing, "Well, *I* thought your paper was just *wonderful,* Randy."

"Me, too," Saralee chimed in.

As luck would have it, Vonna and Saralee sat down at the end of our lunch table. Vonna was doing her usual brag-a-thon. "Oh, Saralee, did I tell you that my mother's dressmaker has the most beautiful material for the princess costume?"

Jeremy piped up. "Don't count your chickens, Vonna. You might not get the lead."

"Not get the lead?" Saralee was shocked. "Of course Vonna will get the lead. Who else would they choose?" She ticked off names on her fingers. "Jennifer Lewis? She's a real ditz. Rosa Carreiro? She's so short, no one would be able to see her. And Megan? Get real." She and Vonna started to giggle.

I kept my cool. "You know, there's an old proverb—"

"Oh, I *hate* those stupid proverbs of yours," Vonna said hotly.

That's another of my little ways to get even with her. I make up these proverbs. They sound deep and wise, but actually they don't make any sense at all. It drives Vonna crazy trying to figure out what they mean.

In a low voice, I said, *"You may travel to the ends of the universe, but the wise man knows that the caged bird will gather no moss."*

Vonna looked bewildered. "What's *that* supposed to mean?"

"It means," said Jeremy, "that it's not over till it's over!"

* * *

The next morning I woke up with the worst cold I'd ever had. My throat ached, my nose was stuffed, and I had a terrible cough.

"Tryouts are only six days from today," I wailed to Daphne. Except she couldn't understand a word I said because I also had laryngitis.

I stayed home from school and lounged around, observing Daphne in action. I had often wondered what she did all day and this was my chance to see for myself.

Poor Daphne—she was so disorganized. She'd start to vacuum, then stop in the middle and do something else, then forget to finish what she started. It didn't help that Aunt Maybelle would keep bugging her every half hour to come and watch different TV programs.

Still, Daphne was a terrific nurse. Which was a good thing since my mother hardly noticed how sick I was. She was too busy running errands and taking care of other people's kids. Daphne kept bringing me juice and aspirin and made me a batch of her "Russian Tea," while I lay on the sofa in the den, feeling miserable and worrying that I might not be better in time for tryouts.

Jeremy brought my homework over after school. He sat on the other side of the room so he wouldn't get any germs, the little wimp.

"Daphne told me you didn't eat any lunch, Megan," he said. "You must *really* be sick."

I was still feeling rotten the next day. "Poor Megan is so bored," Daphne told my sisters. "Why don't you try to perk her up a bit?"

So how did Brenda perk me up? She brought me something to read—her science paper on the solar system! Like I'd really want to curl up with a copy of *that!*

Gina offered to keep me company for a while. She sat there, telling me a long, dull story about her friend, Crystal, who had thought up a special cheer to the tune of "Battle Hymn of the Republic." It was such a boring story I fell asleep in the middle.

By Saturday I was ready to climb the walls with boredom. I was sick of TV, sick of sleeping, sick of reading. And still sick with my cold.

Daphne offered to read to me. I had never heard her do a reading, and it was wonderful. First she read to me from *A Child's Garden of Verses,* and when she came to the poem about "When I was sick and lay abed," I felt like bawling. I had to turn my face away and blow my nose so she wouldn't notice I was crying. It reminded me of when I was a kid and Mom used to read that poem to me.

Then Daphne acted out scenes from different plays. "This is one of my favorites," she said. "It's the scene from *Our Town* where Emily comes back from the dead to relive one day in her life."

For a few moments, I forgot it was Daphne Winston standing there in the den. All I saw was Emily, who had died in childbirth and come back to earth to relive her twelfth birthday. The words pulled at my heart:

> "Do any human beings ever realize life while they live it? . . ."

I grabbed my box of tissues and sobbed my heart out.

Actually, I wasn't only crying for poor Emily. I was also crying for me, Megan Dooley, because I was afraid I might not get better in time for tryouts.

That evening we had a visitor—Bart Peckham. As if I wasn't feeling sick enough!

Ordinarily, Bart would have made some smart remark like, "Isn't it great that Megan has a sore throat and can't talk?"

But that night Bart didn't say a word. He looked extremely depressed. He parked himself at our kitchen table, chin in his hand.

"I haven't heard from Velvet lately," he told Gina glumly. "Maybe it's all over between us. Maybe she found someone better."

"Better than *you?*" I croaked through my stuffed nose, but nobody heard me.

"Maybe Velvet is busy," Gina said, trying to comfort him.

"Maybe Velvet has a lot of homework," Brenda said.

"Maybe Velvet is *sick,"* I said.

Bart sat there complaining for another half hour. Finally he got up from the table. "Well, I guess I'll head home. I don't even feel like going out tonight."

"Cheer up, Bart," Gina said. "Maybe Velvet called you while you were sitting here with us."

"Betcha she *didn't,"* I said. Nobody heard that either.

After Bart left, Brenda said, "I sure wish that girl Velvet would call him. Otherwise, he's going to be over here all the time, moaning and groaning about her."

Brenda had a good point. I knew I had to do something. I waited a few minutes till I knew Bart was home, then went upstairs and phoned him. It wasn't easy to talk with my sore throat and stuffed nose.

He was overjoyed to hear from me.

"I've been sick with a cold," I explained. "That's why I didn't call."

"Yeah," he said. "I figured that was the reason why."

I laughed to myself. Ten minutes earlier at our house, Bart had been driving us all crazy asking, "But why hasn't Velvet called?"

"There's a lot of colds and flu and stuff going around," he went on. "The kid next door has a bad cold, too."

"Oh, really? Who," I asked casually, "is this kid next door?"

"Just a kid named Megan. She's a friend of my sister's."

A friend of Vonna's? That got me so upset I had a terrible fit of coughing.

"Oh, wow, Velvet," Bart said, "you sound as bad as Megan. She can hardly talk." He started to laugh. "Lucky break. That Megan is a little brat."

A little brat, huh?

"That is a *terrible* way to talk about someone," I said in my chilliest voice, and hung up in his ear.

I didn't phone Bart for a couple of days after that. He was miserable and depressed. I knew that because he kept hanging around our house, whining that Velvet had hung up on him, and he didn't know why, and he was worried that she'd never call him again.

Chapter 9

It was like a miracle!

When I woke up on Monday morning, my cold was completely gone. My voice would be okay for tryouts on Tuesday.

At school I discovered Vonna was absent. What good luck! I hoped she had come down with a bad cold, too. But Saralee said that Vonna was staying home from school on purpose, to rest her vocal cords.

"Vonna needs more than a day to rest her vocal cords," Jeremy snorted. "I never heard such an awful voice. It's like a fingernail on a blackboard."

I was getting nervous thinking about tryouts. I kept wishing that Mrs. Thomas, the music teacher who was directing the play, would give us a copy of the script. That way Daphne would be able to coach me on my lines. But all we got was a one-page description of the characters in the play. Mrs. Thomas said it would be too expensive to make photocopies of the script for all the kids who were trying out.

On Tuesday morning Daphne woke me up half an hour earlier than usual so she could blow-dry my hair. At the last minute, I noticed a stain on my pink blouse that hadn't come out in the wash. It was probably from Brenda splattering spaghetti sauce on it.

So I had to make do with my yellow shirt, which is not the best color for me.

You'd think my family would have noticed there was something special going on with me, especially seeing how nice my hair looked. But that morning our house was Crazyville. Mom had gotten an urgent phone call from a client who wanted her to arrange a surprise birthday party that day at noon. Mom was frantically baking her clown cake, while everyone ran around looking for candles and funny party favors.

I didn't want to mess up my hair, so I asked Gina to drive me to school. As I got in the car, I noticed a big glob of pigeon mess on the window.

"Oh, that's *gross,*" I said in disgust.

"No, that's *good,*" Gina insisted. "Mom always says that pigeon poop is supposed to bring good luck."

"Hey, that's right," I said, feeling suddenly happy. It seemed like a lucky omen.

Vonna wasn't in homeroom that morning. I was starting to feel really lucky. Maybe she was sick after all. But then, right before lunch, Vonna showed up.

When I saw her, my stomach felt like someone had made braids in it.

Vonna looked like a princess *ought* to look. Her hair was blonder and curlier than ever, thanks to that beauty salon in Boston. Also, her complexion seemed to glow, although I could swear it was because she was wearing blush and makeup, not because she'd had a facial.

She wore a blue angora sweater, a white skirt, and shoes with little heels. And she had some kind of headband in her hair that looked like a tiara.

At lunch everyone was talking about tryouts. There weren't all that many big parts in the play, except for Princess Leyla, Marvello the Magician, and Klutzella. There were smaller parts for soldiers and ladies-in-waiting.

I heard that some of the girls in our class who'd been planning to try out for the part of Princess Leyla had decided not to bother because they were sure Vonna had it all wrapped up. Instead, they were going to try out for the part of Klutzella. That sure surprised me.

I couldn't believe *anyone* would want the role of Klutzella—she's such a ditzy character.

I had convinced Jeremy to try out for a part as one of the soldiers. I was surprised when he agreed, because he's kind of shy.

The afternoon dragged. A few of the kids told me my hair looked nice, so I felt a little better. To keep calm I did Daphne's breathing exercises.

It was hard to keep my attention on my schoolwork. Instead, I kept looking at the clock. Two hours until tryouts. One hour. Fifteen minutes.

Finally, the bell rang.

"That will be all, Kimberly. Thank you," Mrs. Thomas said. "Next, please."

Mrs. Thomas was sitting at a table in the school auditorium, next to the other judges, Mrs. Caron and Miss Walker, the principal. "Vonna Peckham, you're next," she said with a smile.

Vonna adjusted her headband/tiara as she marched up on stage. She cleared her throat and started to read: "I am the Princess Leyla, and I have need of a magic potion."

All I can say is, Vonna might have looked like a princess, but she sounded like a frog. It wasn't just her voice, it was the way she read. Her words were all bunched together and you could hardly understand what she was saying.

"Now, Vonna dear, slow down a bit," Mrs. Thomas said. "Why don't you try reading those lines again."

That didn't seem fair. Mrs. Thomas was actually coaching Vonna, trying to make her sound better. Nobody else had gotten such royal treatment. In the back of my mind, I remembered that Mrs. Thomas and Vonna's mother were good friends.

I sat there and watched five girls try out for the lead. I thought the judges would never call me, but finally I heard my name.

"Oh, my goodness—*another* one trying out for Princess Leyla?" Mrs. Thomas sounded annoyed. She asked Mrs. Caron to take over running the auditions for a while.

Mrs. Caron handed me the script. "Megan, would you read the part underlined in red?"

I looked at the script. "This is the wrong part," I said. "This is the part of Klutzella."

"Yes, I know," Mrs. Caron said. "We're having people read for one or two different roles." She sat back and smiled encouragingly. "Let's hear you read it, Megan."

It was a scene where Klutzella, the fairy godmother, pretends to be an opera star and talks in a crazy foreign accent. "Don't you know who I am, dollink? I am Madame Maria Caruso von Nightingale—der vorld's greatest soprano!"

I had fun reading the lines because it's a funny scene. Besides, I knew I wasn't trying out for that part, so I wasn't nervous. When I was through, Mrs. Caron smiled and a couple of kids started to clap.

After that I read the part of Princess Leyla. "You must help me, Marvello. My parents have promised me to a prince I have never met . . ."

I don't mean to brag, but I thought I did better than anyone else. Even Jeremy said I was great.

"You sounded like a real princess," he told me on the way home from school.

"Better than Vonna?"

He thought that over. "Vonna *looked* good, but she sounded like she was eating bananas."

"Eating bananas?" I asked, puzzled.

"Yeah—she was talking in bunches," Jeremy said. The two of us laughed all the way home.

I wanted to tell Daphne all about tryouts, but she had gone to the market with Aunt Maybelle. There was nobody else home and I felt like talking to someone, so I decided to phone Bart.

The poor fool was practically overcome with gratitude that I was calling him.

"You know, Velvet," he said hoarsely, "I feel real *close* to you."

"Oh, and I feel close to *you,* too," I said.

Closer than you realize, Bartums!

"You're special," he went on. "I feel like I've known you for a long time."

Oh, you have. Ever since you moved next door.

"So, tell me, Bart," I said, "what's new with your family? How's your sister, Vonna?"

"You see? That's what I mean about you, Velvet. You're really nice. You take an interest in my family."

"Well, that's because I want to know everything about you," I purred. "By the way, didn't Vonna have tryouts today?"

"How'd you know *that?"*

"Oh, Bart, don't you remember? You told me about it the other day." I had to bluff that one.

"I did? Oh, yeah. We talk about so many things, I guess I forgot."

"So how *did* her tryouts go?" I persisted.

Bart made a rude noise. "I don't know and I couldn't care less. My father is furious because my mother spent a fortune on Vonna at some hairdresser in Boston and—"

I heard Daphne and Aunt Maybelle coming up the back steps so I cut the conversation short.

After we finished unpacking the groceries and Aunt Maybelle had hurried off to watch an *Oprah* rerun, Daphne turned to me. "Well, how did tryouts go?"

"Pretty good," I replied. "But we won't know who got the parts until Friday. They're going to post the names on the bulletin board."

"How did Vonna do?"

I giggled. "Vonna sounded awful. She doesn't know a *thing* about public speaking."

Daphne smiled. "Well, it's only three more days until Friday."

"Yeah," I said. "But those three days seem like forever."

Chapter 10

When I got home from school on Friday, Daphne was waiting for me.

"I'm sorry, Megan," she said quietly.

"How did you know?"

"By the sound of your footsteps." She sat down at the kitchen table and made tea.

"I don't even want to talk about it," I said. A moment later everything came pouring out.

"Vonna got the part of Princess Leyla. They picked her because she's pretty, not because she's a good actress." My voice cracked. "It's not *fair.*"

"I know how you feel," Daphne said. "I've had that happen to me. You're right—it's not fair. And it hurts."

We sat there silently, drinking our tea. When I was able to talk again, I said, "The worst thing is, Mrs. Caron put *my* name on the bulletin board for the part of Klutzella."

"Really?" Daphne said. "I didn't know you had tried out for any other part."

"I didn't," I said bitterly. "At tryouts, they asked me to read some of Klutzella's lines, so I did."

"You don't sound very enthusiastic about it," Daphne said.

"I don't *want* that part. Klutzella is the fairy godmother in the play, and she's a real flake. Everybody will laugh at me."

"Are you quite sure of that, Megan?"

"Sure I'm sure. They gave out copies of the script. Here, read it yourself."

Daphne took the script. "Have you already told the teacher that you didn't want the part?"

"No," I said. "I was too embarrassed. Vonna was carrying on, squealing like a pig, when she found out she'd gotten the lead. So I just pretended I was happy about getting the part of Klutzella. I'll tell Mrs. Thomas on Monday that I don't want it."

Daphne settled back in her chair and smoothed out the crumpled script. She was starting to read it when all of a sudden there was the most horrendous screeching coming from the den.

"Hallelujah! Awwkkk. Praise the Lord, you sinners! Squawk. Awwrk. Screech!"

I nearly fell out of my chair. I had never

heard such an awful sound, except for Vonna Mae's voice. "Who's *that?"* I gasped.

Daphne managed a smile. "In all the excitement, I forgot to tell you we have a visitor. One of your mother's clients. Come on, I'll introduce you."

I couldn't believe what I saw.

In the middle of the den was a bright pink birdcage. Inside was a big green parrot, hopping around and squawking loudly.

"What's that bird doing here?" I asked.

"Your mother agreed to parrot-sit for her client, Helen Justley," Daphne said.

"Helen Justley?" I groaned. "Oh, no!" Everyone in town knew Helen Justley. She was a religious fanatic who was always writing letters to the newspaper complaining about young people. She complained that the cheerleaders' skirts were too short, that pierced ears were sinful, and that the students at Winslow High were "going to Hell in a handbasket."

"Repent, you sinner!" the parrot screamed at me.

I sank down on the sofa. It was bad enough I was feeling depressed because I hadn't gotten the lead in the play. Now I had to put up with a mean-looking, religious parrot who smelled as bad as he sounded.

Helen Justley had carefully printed all the

details concerning the care and feeding of her parrot. As I read the sheet of instructions, I snorted.

"His name is *Paul?* What a dumb name for a parrot."

That made him squawk like crazy. He glared at me with those beady little parrot eyes.

I stuck out my tongue at him, and he squawked even louder.

Later that afternoon Aunt Maybelle nearly had a heart attack when she came home from bingo and was greeted by an unearthly screech, *"Sister, you have sinned!"*

Brenda had to put plugs in her ears so she wouldn't be disturbed while she was studying.

And Dad, who hardly ever got upset at anything, was furious when he found out Mom had agreed to keep the bird at our house for two weeks.

"I couldn't say no," Mom told us apologetically. "Poor Helen was called away to her cousin in Texas. She didn't have anyplace to leave the parrot."

"Why couldn't she just leave him in her own house?" Dad demanded. "You could have gone over there to feed him and clean out the cage."

"Helen didn't want Paul to be lonely," Mom said in a small voice.

"Well, you should have checked with us first,"

Dad told her sternly. "Please ask us next time."

Everyone hated that bird. Everyone except Gina. For some reason she and Paul hit it off right away.

"What a darling little birdy you are," Gina crooned when she came home and saw him. She stuck her finger in the cage and Paul didn't even snap at her like he did with everyone else. "Paul want a cracker?"

"Praise the Lord!" the parrot cried joyfully, swinging to and fro.

Aunt Maybelle watched, shaking her head in wonder. "Who would believe one bird could make such an awful smell," she marveled.

"Oh, who's afraid of a little parrot poop?" Gina said gaily. "I don't mind cleaning his cage."

She took Paul down to the basement so he could keep her company while she practiced her cheers.

In all the confusion, I hadn't even had time to think about the play. But later that evening, Jeremy happened to call, and Mom answered the phone. Blabbermouth that he is, Jeremy told her that I had gotten the part of Klutzella.

Mom stared at me in surprise. "Megan, you got a big part in the school play and you didn't even tell us?"

"I don't intend to be in the . . ." I started to say, but Mom kept bombarding me with questions. Before I knew it, I had told her all about Daphne giving me acting lessons.

"My goodness," Mom said with a forced laugh. "I don't even know what goes on in my own house anymore. I never realized you were interested in acting, Megan."

You'd have thought I was starring in some big Hollywood production the way my family carried on.

"We'll all go to see Megan in the play," Dad said. "I can't remember the last time the whole family went somewhere together."

"Jeremy told me he has a part in the play, too," Mom said.

"Oh, big deal," I muttered. "Jeremy is one of the soldiers. He has exactly four words to say."

Aunt Maybelle declared I was entirely too modest. "Can you imagine that—Megan didn't even *tell* anybody she got picked for the part!"

Even Brenda took two minutes from her studying to congratulate me.

I was just about to tell them, once and for all, that I didn't get the part in the play that I really wanted, and I certainly had no intention of playing Klutzella, when Daphne came into the kitchen, waving the script.

"Megan has the best part in the play," Daphne announced. "I've been reading the script and I love it. Klutzella is a wonderful character, warm and funny." She gave me a big smile. "Megan, you're going to be marvelous in it."

If Daphne hadn't used the word marvelous . . .

If Mom hadn't phoned Uncle Jack and his wife to brag . . .

If everybody hadn't made such a big fuss over me . . .

After all that, how could I tell them I wasn't going to be in the play?

And besides that, Daphne wasn't taking "no" for an answer. "Megan, trust me," she said. "This is the kind of challenging role you can really sink your teeth into. It's perfect for you."

"No," I said stubbornly. "The role of Princess Leyla was perfect for me. Only I didn't get it. Vonna did."

"Let me give you a piece of advice that someone gave me years ago," Daphne said. "Whether it's the theater or whether it's life . . . whatever role you get, play it the very best you can."

"Amen, sister!" screeched Paul Parrot as Gina carried him back upstairs into the den.

Chapter 11

I was so busy with rehearsals that the next couple of weeks flew by.

I hated to admit it, but the more I got into the part of Klutzella, the more I liked it. Besides, there was a scene where Klutzella pretends to faint, and it gave me the chance to show everyone how good I was at fainting. Daphne had taught me how to fall so I wouldn't hurt myself.

Mrs. Thomas said I was a natural for comedy roles, so I didn't feel quite as bad about not getting the lead.

Vonna, of course, kept strutting around, bragging and being generally obnoxious. As expected, Randy Howard had gotten the part of Marvello the Magician. I tried not to think about the fact that eventually we would have to rehearse the scene where he kisses Princess Leyla. Then Vonna would really have something to brag about.

At least my life at home was better. Everyone was treating me differently now that I had a big part in the play.

Aunt Maybelle lowered the volume on the TV set when I rehearsed my lines. Gina bragged about me to her cheerleader friends. Even Brenda was nicer. She didn't seem to stay up so late studying and she wasn't making those disgusting noises. Or, if she was, I didn't hear them because I was so tired from rehearsals that I fell asleep as soon as my head hit the pillow every night.

My mother seemed different, too. I know she still felt bad that I hadn't told her Daphne was giving me acting lessons. To tell the truth, I was enjoying all the extra attention from Mom.

Daphne had offered to make my costumes for the play. They were pretty complicated, but that didn't seem to faze her. Daphne may not have been the world's greatest cook or housekeeper, but she was great at sewing.

"That's how I met Edgar," she said dreamily. "I was in a store on Cape Cod looking at sewing machines. Edgar was there on vacation. It was a rainy day and he'd gone shopping with his daughter, Julie. Anyhow, the two of them started asking me questions about sewing machines. That night we all went out to dinner, and the next night Edgar came to see me at the

Falmouth Playhouse. Then we started writing to each other . . ." There was a soft, faraway look in her eyes.

"I don't get it, Daphne," I said. "If you love Edgar so much, what's the problem? Why don't you marry him?"

"It's not that simple. I don't want to wake up some morning and regret that I gave up my acting career." She sighed deeply. "But then again, I don't want to wake up some morning and regret that I gave up marriage, either."

"Repent, you sinner!" Paul Parrot screeched from the other room, and we started to laugh.

"You know," I said, "the best thing about being in the play is that I'm at rehearsals so much, I don't have to listen to that goofy bird squawking all day long."

Gina, however, had gotten very attached to Paul. She always brought him with her whenever she practiced her cheers. And even though she would never even rinse off a dish, Gina didn't seem to mind cleaning Paul's disgusting cage.

"You're more excited over that parrot than you are about going to the senior prom with Greg Walsh," I told her one night at dinner.

"I'm going to miss Paul so much when Mrs. Justley comes back," Gina said, fixing her big brown eyes on my father. "Oh, Daddy, please, can't we get a parrot of our very own?"

"Not in *this* lifetime," he told her. "And not in the next one, either!"

The following day at school, Vonna got an A– on her book report and she made sure everyone knew about it.

"Mrs. Caron hardly *ever* gives more than a B+," Vonna said loudly.

She was still bragging about it on the way to lunch, just in case there might be someone, somewhere in the galaxy, who hadn't heard about that A–.

"Is she sickening, or what?" Jeremy muttered.

". . . and I was just *so* surprised when I saw that A– . . ." Vonna's voice rose suddenly.

I realized why. Randy Howard was coming down the steps, taking them two at a time. Anyone else would probably fall on his face, or look like a jerk, but not Randy. Everything he does is so cool.

Randy bought his lunch, and a few minutes later he sat down at the table next to ours. Along came Vonna and Saralee, trying to figure out where they should sit to be close to Randy. Vonna made a face as she and Saralee plunked themselves down at our table.

"Anyhow, like I was saying, I nearly *fainted* when I saw Mrs. Caron had given me an

A–." Vonna spoke up extra-loud for Randy's benefit.

It was just too much. She was ruining my lunch.

I put my hand up close to my mouth like a microphone. *"A little louder for our West Coast audience, Vonna,"* I boomed out. *"They can't quite hear you in San Diego."*

Jeremy and the other kids at our table broke up.

Vonna glared at me. She tossed her curls and turned to Saralee. "Oh, remember that girl, Velvet, I told you about? The one who's got a crush on my brother? Well, he's going to invite her to see me in the play."

"You mean the girl who's going to be a model?" Saralee asked breathlessly. "Oh, wow, I'd like to meet her."

"You'll get to meet her all right," I said in a low voice.

But the only one who heard me was Jeremy.

When I got home from rehearsal, I decided to call Bart. I'd been so busy I hadn't talked to him in a few days. And I had to keep stringing him along until the night of the play.

There was so much noise on his end I could barely hear him. "What's going on at your house?" I asked.

"Oh, that's Vonna." Bart sounded disgusted. "What a spoiled brat. She's carrying on because my mother refused to write another book report for her."

Another book report? My ears perked up. "Do you mean your mother writes book reports for your sister?"

"Well, sure," he said. "She does them for me, too. Except right now she's too busy. My mother was an English major. In fact," he added, "Vonna even got an A on a book report she brought home today."

"You mean an A–," I started to say, then caught myself in time. This was my chance to get some inside dirt on Vonna.

"Your sister has such an unusual name," I said sweetly. "How did she ever get a name like 'Vonna'?"

Bart chuckled. "She'd kill me if she knew I told anyone. My parents named her after this rich old aunt of my mother's, Vonna Mae Bumpus."

"Vonna Mae Bumpus?" I smothered a laugh. This would be good ammunition. I could hear it all now.

Vonna: Well, if it isn't Klutzy Klutzella.
Me: Well, if it isn't Vonna Mae.
Jeremy: Vonna may *what?*
Me: Vonna may bump us.

"My mother figured old Auntie Vonna would be so happy about her namesake that she'd leave us all her money when she croaked," Bart went on.

"And did she? Leave you all her money, I mean?"

"Are you kidding?" He snorted. "The old witch left all her money to the Winslow Animal Shelter. Can you believe it?"

"Awww, that's rotten," I said in my most sympathetic voice. "And there was poor little Vonna, stuck with that awful name."

"Yeah, my sister hates her name," Bart agreed. "But let's not talk about her. Let's talk about us. When am I going to meet you?"

"Well, it's awfully hard to get out of the house with my parents being so strict," I said. "But there *is* one night they won't be home and I could get out for a while. It's a Friday, May 24th."

"Hey, I think that's the night of Vonna's play," Bart said excitedly. "In fact, she asked me to invite you. It starts about seven o'clock."

"Oh, that's too early, " I hedged. "My parents will still be home. But I could probably meet you later on, after the play. Maybe we could go somewhere for pizza."

"Fan-*tas*-tic!" Bart cried. "I know this great place—Pizza Heaven. Everyone goes there. It's on Elm Street near the mall. How does ten o'clock sound?"

"It sounds perfect, Bart," I said in my most Velvety voice. "Just perfect."

Bart sighed. "Yeah, but it seems like a long time to wait. Why can't I meet you sooner than—"

I was getting sick and tired of his constant whining. "Ooops, I've got to go now." I hung up the phone and went downstairs to help Daphne with dinner.

As I set the table, I could hear Gina in the basement, practicing her cheer:

Winslow High, you're the best.

You stand out from all the rest.

Every so often, Paul Parrot would accompany her with a loud squawk.

"One thing about Gina," Daphne observed, "she's *dedicated*."

"I think the word is *weird*," I said.

Look to the east, look to the west.

Winslow High, you're the best!

Suddenly, Gina let out a shriek. A few seconds later, she came bounding up the stairs into the kitchen. At first I was hoping that maybe she had done a somersault and smothered Paul Parrot, but no such luck. She was clutching his pink cage and he was very much alive.

"You won't *believe* this!" Gina cried, her eyes shining. "Paul, show them."

Paul turned his oversized parrot head toward me. In a perfect imitation of Gina, he screeched: *"Winslow High, you're the best!"*

Daphne's jaw dropped. So did the silverware I was putting on the table.

"You stand out from all the rest!" Paul screeched, even louder than before.

Gina was delirious with joy. "Isn't that *awesome?"* She tickled Paul's beak. "You are the best little birdy-wirdy in the whole world," she cooed.

"You're the best! Awwk. You're the best!"

"Isn't it wonderful?" Gina said, beaming proudly. "Just think—a cheerleading parrot!"

"I'm not sure the world is ready for that," I said.

"Wait till Mommy and Daddy hear him. What do you suppose they'll say, Megan?"

Paul Parrot answered for me. *"Rah, Rah!"* he screeched.

Chapter 12

"That was very good, Megan," Mrs. Thomas said. "Just work on making your voice sound completely different in the scene where Klutzella pretends to be Princess Irene."

She turned to Randy Howard. "You're doing fine, but you need to work on memorizing your lines, Randy."

He nodded. Most of the time, Randy is quiet and shy. But whenever he's in a play, he seems to come out of his shell. It's amazing how he manages to turn into loud, fast-talking Marvello the Magician.

Mrs. Thomas stood up. "And Vonna," she said wearily, "you need to practice projecting your voice so the audience can hear you."

That was the strangest thing. Normally, Vonna's voice is loud and shrill. But whenever she was playing Princess Leyla, you could hardly hear her.

As we got ready to leave, Mrs. Thomas reminded us that rehearsal would be at three-thirty sharp the next day. "Don't forget—the play is only a week away," she said.

As if we could forget!

The play was all everyone was talking about. There was such a demand for tickets that the school had to set a limit of three tickets per student. Mom and Dad had been upset because we needed five tickets so the whole family could see the play. Luckily, Jeremy's parents had a computer show that night, so Jeremy told us we could have their tickets.

When I got home that afternoon, Daphne was busy working on my costumes. One of them had all kinds of sequins that had to be sewn on by hand. That took a lot of time, so she was doing less and less housekeeping. Considering how little she was doing in the first place, I thought it was a miracle that she managed to keep her job. I was pleasantly surprised to find out that Brenda and Aunt Maybelle had been pitching in to help her with the housework.

Watching Daphne, I asked, "How did you learn to sew like that?"

"Self-defense. I had to learn how to fix my costumes," she said. "And once when I was between acting jobs, I took a sewing course. But tell me, Megan, how did rehearsal go today?"

I told Daphne what Mrs. Thomas had suggested about making my voice sound completely different in the Princess Irene scene. "How do you think I could do that?"

Daphne bit off a piece of thread. "You might try doing that scene with a British accent."

"Hey, that's a good idea." I practiced the scene that way and it seemed to work. Daphne went upstairs to use Mom's sewing machine while I stayed in the den, perfecting my accent.

Then I had a brainstorm.

Why not test out the accent to see if it really *did* sound different than my usual voice?

And who better to test it out on than old Wilfred Boggs?

I had played enough telephone tricks on him so that by now he ought to be able to recognize my voice. Let's see if I could fool him once again with my British accent!

He answered the phone, sounding delighted, as usual, that someone had called him.

"Mr. Boggs," I trilled, sounding as British as I could, "we are conducting a survey, and I wonder if you'd be jolly good enough to answer some questions."

"Why, surely," he said. "I'd be pleased to."

"Yes, well," I continued, "what are your three favorite television shows?"

There was a long pause. "Oh, I'm sorry," he

said after a while. "I don't watch television."

"Oh, you don't care for the *telly,* Mr. Boggs?" That sounded quite British I thought.

"It's not that—" he started to say. I heard a click as if someone had picked up the phone.

"Oh, was that your wife?" I asked.

"No," he said quietly. "My wife passed away a few years ago."

That made me feel bad. "Well, Mr. Boggs, I'm sorry to have bothered you. Thanks for your help, old chap."

No sooner had I hung up the telephone than Daphne came flying down the stairs, an angry look on her face.

"Megan, why were you calling Wilfred Boggs?" she demanded.

"How'd you know *that?"* I gasped.

"Because I happened to pick up the phone just now to call the fabric store. And I heard you playing a cruel trick on a lovely man."

"You mean you *know* Wilfred Boggs?"

"I certainly do. I know him through the Guild for the Blind. He's one of the clients I make those recordings for."

"He's *blind?"* I practically choked. "Honest, Daphne, I didn't know that. I just happened to pick his name out of the phone book one time. And I kept calling him up because he always seemed to fall for everything."

I had never seen Daphne so angry. "Well, that solves the mystery," she said. "Mr. Boggs told me he had been getting some prank calls."

She sat down on the sofa. "Let me explain something. Blind people feel very isolated. Sometimes, just hearing a voice on the telephone means a lot—even if that voice is playing a prank."

I felt like the rat of the century. "I didn't mean any harm. If I'd known—"

"That's why I'm a volunteer reader," Daphne went on. "Years ago, an elderly blind woman came up to me after a performance and said how much she enjoyed the sound of my voice. And she told me something else I'd never realized. Many blind people wish that someone would phone them every now and then and read them items from the newspaper. A little thing like that means so much."

I held out my arm. "Here—take my blood. Put a knife in me." I tried to make a joke because I felt so guilty.

Daphne put down my costume. "Megan," she said gently, "you have a wonderful, magical voice. But you should use it to *help* people, not hurt them."

I swallowed. "Would you tell Mr. Boggs I'm sorry?"

She gave me a thoughtful look. "I've got a better

idea. Maybe you could offer to phone him now and then and read to him from the newspaper.

"Are you kidding?" I cried. "I can't call him back. I'd die of embarrassment."

"Well, think abut it," Daphne said. "It would be good for both of you."

For the next few days, I kept myself busy with rehearsals and schoolwork so I wouldn't have to think about Wilfred Boggs.

When I walked in the house one afternoon, a pleasant surprise awaited me. Paul Parrot was gone. Helen Justley was back in town and had rushed over from the airport to retrieve her fine-feathered friend.

"Well," I said when I heard the good news, "as Paul himself used to say, '*hallelujah!*'"

I was so happy, in fact, that I decided to do a good deed. I was going to read the newspaper to Wilfred Boggs. Daphne immediately called him and explained everything.

"He's looking forward to hearing from you, Megan," she told me.

So after dinner I took the *Winslow Dispatch* into the den and phoned him. I felt embarrassed at first, but he was very nice.

"Which part of the paper do you want me to read?" I asked. "The front page? The sports section?"

"If you don't mind, I'd like you to read me the stock quotations."

Have you ever looked at the pages in the newspaper with the stock quotations?

I never had before. There's so much tiny print and so many figures, it could make you dizzy. I didn't even know how to read it aloud.

Mr. Boggs explained how. "As I recall, you read the figures across. It tells the highest price the stock has been, and the lowest price, and what it is now."

I started to read. And kept on reading.

Not only was it dull, it went on forever. "NYNEX—699 1/8 . . ." I thought my voice would give out.

Finally, I had to tell him I needed to stop because I had to save my voice for the play. He apologized for keeping me talking on the phone so long.

"I guess you must own a lot of stocks and bonds," I said.

"Oh, no," he said. "I don't own any at all."

"You don't own any stocks and bonds? Then how come you asked me to read the stock quotations page?"

"Because," said Wilfred Boggs happily, "I like hearing your voice. You've got such a lovely voice, Megan."

* * *

I had just finished my homework when the doorbell rang. I heard Dad greet someone, and then I heard a woman yelling hysterically.

I rushed out to see what was going on.

There in the foyer stood Helen Justley. She looked furious. Her thin gray hair stuck up in spikes, her eyes bulged, and her face was the color of an overripe tomato.

"I ought to sue you for what you've done!" she cried. "The authorities will hear about this!"

Mom was bewildered. "What are you talking about?"

"You know perfectly well what I'm talking about." Helen Justley shook a big, black umbrella threateningly. "You brainwashed my poor little bird!"

"Now, now, Mrs. Justley," Dad started to say, but she cut him short.

"I had a decent, God-fearing parrot, and you turned him into a—a *cheerleader!*" Helen Justley practically spat the word out.

"I taught Paul to say things like 'Praise the Lord' and 'Hallelujah,'" she continued. "But what happened? Two weeks in this house and you poisoned his mind. Now all he says is 'Winslow High, you're the best' or 'Rah, Rah!'"

She shook her umbrella at Gina. "And it's all *your* fault, missy—you with your short skirts and your pierced ears—"

Gina burst out crying.

Mom stepped forward, eyes blazing. "How *dare* you talk to my family that way. Let me remind you, Helen, you practically *begged* me to take that noisy, nasty bird into my home. Gina was the one who fed him and played with him and cleaned his cage. But this is *not*—I repeat, *not*—a finishing school for parrots! We are not responsible for Paul's vocabulary."

Helen Justley drew herself up to her full height of four foot ten.

"I will *never* again use the services of Let Mama Do It. Furthermore, I have no intention of paying you the balance of what I owe."

With that she stormed out of the house.

Mom looked dazed. "I can't believe it. After all I've done for that woman. I've driven her to revival meetings, and I've typed those crazy letters she writes to the newspaper. I've done so many errands for her, and she owes me a lot of money."

"Maybe this finally shows you something, Annie," Dad said gently. "You need to do some serious thinking about your business."

"What do you mean?" Mom asked.

"Well, speaking as your accountant—and your husband—I have to say I think you're doing too much for too many people and getting too little for it—in money or appreciation."

He put his arm around her. "Hon, you have to weed out people like Helen Justley. For the amount of time and effort you put in, it's not cost-effective. You've got to set priorities."

"Priorities," Mom said slowly. "That's the key word. I've been doing a lot of thinking about priorities lately. And I realize now that I've been so busy doing things for everyone else that I've neglected what's most important to me: all of you. I didn't even know Megan was trying out for the school play . . ." Her voice trailed off to a whisper.

"Oh, hey, Mom, that's okay," I said. I had wanted her to feel guilty, but now that she did, it made *me* feel bad, too.

Dad smiled at Mom. "Annie, girl, you just have to set limits, that's all. You know what they say—moderation in all things."

"I just don't know what to do anymore, Bill. I *want* to cut down on my hours. I *want* to spend more time at home." Mom's lips trembled. "But I also want to keep my business going. And I'm afraid that if I have to turn down a client's request, they might not call me again."

We all trooped into the kitchen, where Daphne was making tea.

My brain was in high gear. I kept thinking about what Mom had just said. She was trying to balance her career and her family, and it wasn't easy.

I'd never realized it before, but now that I'd gotten so interested in acting, I could understand how your work can be really important to you.

And I could feel another brilliant idea coming!

"You know, Mom," I said hesitantly, "maybe we could help you."

Everyone turned to stare at me.

"Well," I went on, "remember the other day when you had to pick up someone at the train station and you were also supposed to help Mr. Benson's son with his arithmetic?"

Mom nodded. "Oh, that was such an awful day. I had so many things to do at the same time."

"I know," I said. "But maybe you could have had Brenda tutor Jeffrey Benson instead. Brenda's a math whiz."

Brenda glanced at me in surprise. "Yeah," she said, "I would have done it."

"And the time you had to stay with Mrs. Gold's mother-in-law when she came out of the hospital," Aunt Maybelle piped up. "I could have helped you out."

Dad look pleased. "You see, Annie? There's plenty of talent right here in this family. We could all pitch in now and then and give you a hand. Just ask us."

Gina wiped her eyes, which were still red from crying. "I could help out, too." She sniffled. "I could teach kids to do cheers and somersaults."

"Plus she's great with parrots," I pointed out.

Mom stirred her tea, a frown creasing her forehead. "There's just one problem. If you're all helping me, then the name of my business won't fit anymore. How can I call it Let Mama Do It if I have everyone else in the family helping me?"

She sighed. "It's such a *catchy* name. And it's gotten so much good publicity, too."

"You'd need a different name," Dad agreed. "Hmmm. Let's see. What else could you call it?"

Everyone was silent, trying to think up a clever new name for Mom's business.

It came to me in a flash.

"I've got it!" I cried excitedly. "How about calling the business *Let The Dooleys Do It!*"

Chapter 13

Dress rehearsal was a horror.

I forgot my lines. Randy Howard had a laughing fit and refused to rehearse the kissing scene. Vonna missed her cues and kept sneezing.

She was in such a rotten mood that she stuck her foot out and tripped me. Vonna is very spiteful that way.

Jeremy was indignant. "Everyone saw what she did," he said on the way home. "Aren't you *mad?"*

"Not me," I said. "You know my motto: Don't get mad—get even!"

Vonna and Saralee were walking in back of us, giggling away as usual.

"Look at who's in front of us," Vonna cried shrilly. "It's Klutzella Klutz and Jeremy Jerk!"

"Look at who's in back of us. It's Vonna Dance and Saralee Suck-up!" Jeremy said without missing a beat.

The two of them were speechless.

I clapped Jeremy on the back. "Way to go, Jer. You're getting pretty good with the comebacks."

He grinned. "I had a good teacher."

We walked along listening to Vonna tell Saralee how excited Bart was about meeting Velvet after the play. "He bought her a dozen red roses," Vonna bragged. "They're in our refrigerator."

Jeremy nudged me. "You hear that?"

"Yeah," I said. "And you can bet Bart's face will be as red as those roses when he finds out who Velvet is!"

When I came into the house, Daphne was at the ironing board, putting the finishing touches on my costumes. I told her how awful dress rehearsal had been.

"Don't worry. Things like that always happen at dress rehearsal," she reassured me. "Everything will be fine tomorrow night, you'll see." She held up the costume I wore in the last act. "What do you think of this?"

"Oh, wow," I said admiringly. "That's fantastic." The costume was in layers. The final layer was the beautiful dress Klutzella wears in the last act when she reveals to Princess Leyla that she's her fairy godmother.

"Yes, it did come out nicely, didn't it?" Daphne stood back to admire her handiwork.

"And how do you like Klutzella's magic wand? Brenda made it. She did a lovely job, don't you think?"

"Brenda? She made this—for me?" I examined the sparkly, silver wand. It was perfect. "Say, what's *with* Brenda anyhow? Did she fall on her head or something? How come she's being so nice to me lately?"

"Maybe it's because you're being nice to her," Daphne observed. "It's a two-way street."

"It's not that I'm being nice to Brenda," I decided. "It's just that I've been so busy lately I haven't had time to *fight* with her."

Daphne shut off the iron. "Megan, you've just stumbled onto one of life's secrets. When you're busy with something you love, you feel *good* about yourself. And when you feel good about yourself, you don't need to sweat the small stuff. And that," she said with a smile, "is why people like being around people who are busy."

I mulled that over. Daphne just might have something there. A couple of days earlier, I had been talking with Patti Rogers, who sat next to me in homeroom. I happened to mention how busy I was, giving Mom ideas for Let The Dooleys Do It and reading to Wilfred Boggs over the phone. Not to mention rehearsing for the play, too.

Patti was impressed. "Wow, you do such interesting things," she said enviously. And then she did something she'd never done before.

She invited me over to her house. I told her I was just too busy.

And then yesterday she practically begged me to come to the sleep-over party she was having a week after the play.

Nobody had ever invited me to a sleep-over party before, either!

That night we were all sitting at the kitchen table eating frozen yogurt and watching Gina model her prom gown when the telephone rang.

Daphne answered it and her face turned pale. She excused herself and hurried into the den to use the extension.

"I'll bet that's her gentleman friend, Edgar," Aunt Maybelle whispered.

With a start I remembered that Daphne had a big decision to make. She would have to give Edgar her answer in a day or so.

Then I also realized that whatever she decided, Daphne was going to be leaving us. I could feel my throat tighten up. I would really miss her. For the first time in my life, I would actually be *sorry* to see a housekeeper go!

When Daphne returned Mom came right out

and asked what her decision was going to be.

"Oh, dear, I'm still not sure." Daphne sat down heavily. "I do love Edgar. But would it be fair to marry him? Would I like living in a small town? Would I get along with his children?"

"Of course you will." Mom patted Daphne's hand. "You've gotten used to living here in Winslow and it's smaller than Swansea. And don't forget, you'll be near Boston and Providence and Newport."

"And less than an hour from New York by plane," Dad put in.

"Edgar's children will *love* you," Aunt Maybelle predicted.

"If you can get along with Megan, you can get along with anyone," Brenda said, but not in a mean way. Everyone laughed and so did I.

Daphne stared at her melted yogurt. "Ah," she said softly, "but how will I fill my time? And the real issue—will I miss the theater?"

"You've been here nearly three months and gotten along just fine without the theater," I pointed out.

Daphne shook her head. "Not really. All this time I've been working with you on your play, Megan, and that's one of the things that has kept me happy while I've been here. I definitely need regular contact with the theater one way or another." She glanced up at us and gave an embarrassed smile. "Goodness knows, I'm not cut out to be a housekeeper."

We all laughed. Then suddenly, I sat bolt upright in my chair.

"Daphne, you're terrific at teaching," I burst out. "Why don't you open a drama school in Swansea? You could give acting lessons and put on plays."

Nobody said a word. They just looked at me.

"And maybe Edgar's kids could help you," I babbled on. "You could call it Daphne's Drama School or something. That way you could marry Edgar, but you'd still be in the theater, sort of, and—"

Daphne's eyes filled with tears. "What a wonderful idea, Megan. You're right. I could give lessons, not just to young people, but to anybody who wants to learn about acting. There are lots of older people interested in amateur theater."

"*I* always wanted to be an actress," Aunt Maybelle said wistfully. "I wish you were opening a drama school here in Winslow."

Who would have believed Aunt Maybelle was a frustrated actress?

Daphne jumped up from her chair and rushed to the den. "I'm going to call Edgar right now and tell him what I've decided!"

"Why don't you tell Edgar we've got an extra

ticket for the play tomorrow night," Mom called after her. "Maybe he'll want to drive up here."

Ten minutes later Daphne came back, a big smile on her face.

"Edgar thinks the idea of the drama school is wonderful. We're going to set the wedding date and continue talking about the school. Oh, and yes, he's coming to the play tomorrow night."

She came over and hugged me. "I think everything is going to work out, thanks to you, Megan."

Mom hugged me, too. "You're *marvelous,* Megan."

I didn't think I had heard right. "What did you just say?"

She smiled. "I said you're marvelous, Megan."

"You sure are," Dad agreed.

My throat tightened up again. *Marvelous Megan!* That was how I had wanted my parents to think of me back when I was planning to try out for the part of Princess Leyla.

I hadn't gotten that part. And they hadn't seen me in the play yet.

But, even so, they *still* thought of me as *Marvelous Megan!*

Chapter 14

And then, all of a sudden, it was the night of the play.

Backstage, everybody was nervous.

What made us even more nervous was the fact that Vonna hadn't shown up. Everyone in the cast was supposed to be at school at least an hour before the play started. Mrs. Thomas kept calling Vonna's house, but there was no answer. We were all frantic, wondering what had happened.

Finally, twenty minutes before curtain time, Vonna waltzed in. It seemed her mother didn't think the teachers would do a good enough job with the makeup, so she had taken Vonna to a special cosmetics salon.

I had to admit Vonna looked really pretty, and the blue gown her mother had had specially made in Boston was beautiful. Vonna made sure everyone knew how much it cost.

As the auditorium started filling up, I could feel my stomach churning. Jeremy kept peeking out and giving me reports on who was in the audience.

"Your family just came in. Oh, there's Daphne with some tall, skinny guy. That must be Edgar," he said.

I was getting a serious case of stage fright. I was standing there, chewing my fingernails and trying to do some deep-breathing exercises, when I heard someone whisper, "Pssst, Megan."

It was Brenda. "You're not supposed to be backstage," I whispered.

"Here, take this for good luck." She put something in my hand and scooted off.

I stared in amazement. It was Brenda's lucky silver dollar. She always carried it with her when she had a test at school. A couple of times I had asked if I could borrow it, figuring maybe some of her brains and good luck might rub off on me when I had a test. But Brenda would never let me have it.

Now she was actually lending it to me and I hadn't even asked!

I put the silver dollar in my shoe. And, just like that, the jittery feeling in my stomach vanished.

"Five minutes to curtain!" Mrs. Thomas announced.

I threw back my shoulders and took a deep breath. I was ready.

From the moment I made my entrance as Klutzella, I felt as if the audience was completely with me.

They laughed and clapped in all the right places. When the curtain went down after the first act, there was a lot of applause.

Now I could understand why Daphne loved acting so much. I was having such a great time onstage that I didn't feel the least bit nervous.

Backstage, Mrs. Thomas whispered to me, "Megan, you were wonderful!"

In Act Two, Vonna had trouble remembering her lines and she stumbled over some of her words. To make matters worse, you could hardly hear her. People in the audience kept yelling, *"Louder, louder!"*

I was glad Daphne had taught me all those special exercises and techniques. I didn't have any problem at all projecting my voice.

Speaking of voices, the funniest thing happened near the end of the second act. Jeremy only had four words to say: "Halt, who goes there?" But right in the middle, his voice changed. He started off in his usual high, squeaky voice, but ended up in this deep, booming voice.

The audience broke up.

Jeremy was pretty cool about it. He just grinned and gave a little bow, and the play went on.

Right after that was the part where Klutzella pretends to be Princess Irene. It's a hilarious scene, and the whole auditorium rocked with laughter.

"You're the hit of the show, Megan," one of the teachers whispered to me afterward.

The third act went smoothly, although Vonna flubbed a couple of her lines.

And then came the big scene where Marvello the Magician kisses Princess Leyla as he tries to rouse her from the magic spell that has been cast over her. You could hear a pin drop in the auditorium.

"Give me a sign, oh Princess Leyla, that you are only sleeping," Randy cried dramatically as he bent down to kiss her.

At that moment, Vonna sneezed loudly.

And kept on sneezing.

Not just little sneezes, but great big, wet sneezes that sprayed everyone onstage. Including Randy.

"Oh, *gross!"* he cried, wiping his face.

The audience roared. So did the whole cast. Everyone, that is, except Vonna.

Finally, the auditorium quieted down. After

the final scene, where Klutzella reveals that she is the fairy godmother, the audience burst into deafening applause.

They were still clapping and cheering and whistling when the curtain went down.

Daphne had once told me that applause is the most beautiful sound in the world, and she was right. I got the loudest applause of all, plus the most curtain calls. I heard someone in the audience yelling, "Bravo, bravo!" I think it was my father.

Backstage was a blur of excitement. People were hugging me and shaking my hand and telling me how great I was.

My family elbowed their way through the crowd, with big smiles on their faces. Daphne was clutching Edgar's arm. She introduced us. Edgar was pleasant-looking but certainly not handsome, the way Daphne had described him.

"You were just great, Megan," Edgar said, pumping my hand. "All I can say is, if you're any indication, Daphne will be very successful with her drama school."

I decided Edgar was better-looking than I had thought.

The plan was for all of us to go to Pizza Heaven afterward. But I wanted to go home and change out of my costume first so I would be comfortable.

"Why don't you guys go ahead and get a table?" I told my parents. "Daphne and Edgar can drive me back to the house."

I still had one more role to play that night—Velvet, the girl with the emerald eyes!

Edgar waited downstairs while Daphne helped me out of my costume. She gave me some special cold cream to take off my makeup.

Then she sat down on Brenda's bed and said, "Well, Megan, what are you planning to do about Bart?"

I was stunned. "How did *you* know?"

Daphne didn't answer.

"I bet Jeremy told you, didn't he?" I cried hotly. "Well, Bart Peckham has it coming. I'm going to embarrass him in front of his friends when they find out *I'm* Velvet."

"Please listen to me, Megan," Daphne said. "You'll do more than embarrass Bart. You'll humiliate him. If Velvet didn't show up tonight, Bart would be embarrassed. But if you tell everyone that Velvet is really Megan Dooley, Bart would be humiliated. Think about it—do you really want to humiliate anyone?"

Daphne was spoiling everything!

"Bart deserves to be humiliated. He told me I couldn't act my way out of a paper bag. He called me a little brat." My voice rose in anger. "Bart and Vonna have been putting me down since I was a little kid. Well, tonight I'm *really* going to show them!"

"You already *did* show them," Daphne said softly. "You showed them you're bright and talented. You were the star of the show."

I covered my ears, not wanting to hear her. "I've always said I don't get mad—I get even. Well, tonight I'm going to get even, all right. I'm finally getting my revenge."

Daphne came over and put her arm around me. "Do you know the best way to get even, Megan? By making yourself so darn terrific that you don't *need* to get even with anyone. That's the best revenge of all."

For some reason that made me start to cry.

"I wanted to get rid of you," I confessed to Daphne. "I was only using you at first because you gave me acting lessons. But after tryouts, I was planning to . . ." I couldn't finish because I was crying so hard.

"I knew that," Daphne said. "And it doesn't matter. Because you and I became friends." She smiled at me. "Megan, I'm going to miss you."

"Me, too." I pulled away from her and hurried to the bathroom to splash my face with cold water.

I felt a whole lot better after my confession

to Daphne. But that didn't mean I agreed with her about Bart. I still intended to get even with him. I could just picture him, looking at his watch as he waited for Velvet at Pizza Heaven.

In fact, I could picture the whole scene in my mind. I would saunter over to his table. And in my best Velvet voice, I would say, "Oh, Bartums, I *do* believe those roses are for me."

And then I'd tell his friends that *I* was Velvet, and that I had been fooling him all this time. Maybe I'd even tell some of the stuff Bart had confided in me. They'd laugh their heads off.

And Bart would be mortified!

But as I patted my face dry, I glanced at myself in the mirror and a funny feeling came over me. It was as if I had never really seen myself before.

It got me all confused.

"Are you ready to go, Megan?" Daphne called from downstairs.

"I'm ready," I told her.

Chapter 15

Pizza Heaven was packed.

It seemed like everyone who had been in the audience was there, not to mention everyone who had been in the cast. Dad stood up and waved us over to a big table in the corner.

People were smiling and pointing at me. As I walked past a booth, somebody whispered, "That's the girl who played Klutzella. She was terrific!"

"Well, here's our celebrity." Mom was beaming. "Everyone's been coming over to tell us how great you were in the play."

As if on cue, two people I didn't even know came over and said, "Hey, you were *great* in the play."

I sat down next to Jeremy. "You're a fink," I muttered. "Why did you tell Daphne about Bart?"

Jeremy shrugged. "I don't know. I guess I felt sorry for him."

I gawked at Jeremy. "How come you're talking in that low voice? Talk in your real voice."

"This *is* my real voice," he told me smugly. "I guess I reached puberty."

I rolled my eyes to the ceiling. "Well, pardon *me,* Mister Macho."

Someone tapped me on the shoulder. It was Randy Howard. "You were real good, Megan," he mumbled, then rushed off before I could say a word.

Another tap on the shoulder. This time it was Saralee, wanting me to autograph the program for her kid brother. After she left I whispered to Jeremy, "That name you gave her was perfect. Saralee really *is* a little suck-up."

I got myself settled and glanced around the room. Sure enough, a few tables away sat Bart Peckham and a couple of his friends. He was clutching a bouquet of wilted roses and he kept looking at the door anxiously as he waited for Velvet to show up.

Daphne and Jeremy were watching me. My heart started to pound and there was a roaring in my ears.

Go ahead, said a little voice. *Get even with Bart!*

But then I thought about what Daphne had said earlier and I got all mixed up. What should I do? Tell Bart I was Velvet? Not tell Bart?

I pushed my chair away from the table and stood up. "Excuse me a sec. I'll be right back." I walked slowly over to where Bart was sitting.

Daphne and Jeremy swiveled their heads around.

Taking a deep breath, I said, "Hey, Bart, I've got something to tell you."

He stopped talking to his friends and looked at me. "Yeah? What's up?"

"Well, when I was at my house, changing out of my costume, a girl rang our doorbell. She said nobody was home at your house and she needed to get an important message to you." I paused. "She said her name was Velvet."

"Velvet!" Bart sat up as if someone had stuck a pin in him. "What did she say? What message?"

"She said she was supposed to meet you here tonight, only she can't make it."

"She can't make it?" Bart choked. "Why not?"

"Because," I said, racking my brain for an answer, "she—uh—she had to leave right away for private school in Switzerland."

"Switzerland? Velvet's going to *Switzerland?"* Bart looked like he was about to cry.

"Yeah, but it's only for five years or so," I went on. "Anyhow, she told me to tell you she can't write to you because her parents found out she likes you and they're very, very strict."

Angie the Airhead

by Mary Towne

Angie has always enjoyed spending the summer with her family at a holiday camp in Vermont. This year, though, Angie has a big problem. She's "borrowed" money from the treasury of her baton-twirling club back home, and she's desperate to replace the cash before anyone notices it's missing. But no one at the camp will offer scatterbrained Angie a job. Stung by not being taken seriously by anyone—even her own family!—Angie vows to make people see her in a new light. Can Angie the Airhead ever really change?

Smiling proudly, Gina raised her pompoms in a signal and the girls began to chant:

Megan Dooley, you're the best.

You stand out from all the rest.

They did some cute little steps, kicking to the left, then to the right.

Look to the East, look to the West.

They waved their pompoms up and down, up and down, then cradled them against their faces.

Megan Dooley, you're the best!

Everyone in the restaurant applauded wildly. It was a moment I would never forget.

My parents were beaming so brightly I swear they could glow-in the dark.

Gina had finally created the perfect cheer—and it was for me!

I couldn't talk because there was a lump in my throat the size of a tennis ball.

Otherwise, I would have told her, "Hey, Gina—your pompom has been dragging in Brenda's spaghetti and you've got marinara sauce all over your face!"

"Why are you giving them to me?" I asked. "Why not give them to your mother or Vonna?"

"Are you kidding? They'd throw the roses in my face," Bart declared. "I think maybe it was the roses that made Vonna sneeze. I got them on sale a couple of days ago and she's been sneezing ever since."

There was something about getting a bouquet of red roses—even if they were half-dead—that made me feel like a Broadway star.

I was touched. *"Oh, Bart!"* I said.

He gave me a strange look.

"What's the matter?" I asked.

"For a minute there, you sounded like—oh, never mind." Bart walked away, shaking his head.

The waitress brought our pizzas and Brenda's plate of spaghetti. I hadn't realized how hungry I was. I had just polished off my third slice of pizza when I heard a commotion.

There in the doorway of Pizza Heaven stood my sister, Gina, and some of her cheerleader friends. They were dressed in their cheerleader outfits and carrying their white pompoms.

Gina came over and stood by our table while the other cheerleaders lined up nearby.

Everyone stared. Conversation in the restaurant came to a halt. People sat there frozen, holding slices of pizza in midair.

everybody having pizza?" Dad asked above the clank of dishes.

I was feeling noble. "Dad," I said, "Brenda doesn't really care for pizza. I think she'd rather have spaghetti with marinara sauce."

Brenda flashed me a smile. At least I think it was a smile. Maybe it was just the light reflecting off her retainer.

Daphne and Edgar were holding hands and discussing wedding plans with my parents. Jeremy was showing off his new deep voice, talking about computers.

And Aunt Maybelle announced that she just might try out for the Senior Sweetheart Pageant at the Council on Aging.

Someone was missing. "Hey, where's Gina?" I asked. "Didn't she come to the play?"

"Oh, yes," Mom assured me. "Gina saw the play with us and thought you were fantastic. But she said she had something important to do afterward, so she couldn't come with us."

"Hah!" I muttered in disgust. "I might have known. Gina is so *selfish*. You'd think, just for once, she could do something to make *me* feel good, instead of hanging out with her friends."

Another tap on my shoulder. I looked up to see Bart Peckham, thrusting the roses at me. "Here—you might as well have these," h
"I was going to give them to Velvet."

I was about to return to my table when Bart grabbed my arm. "Listen, Megan," he said urgently, "what did Velvet look like? Was she—" He couldn't get the words out.

I knew what he wanted to hear. The most important thing of all.

"Velvet," I said, "had long blond hair. And emerald eyes."

"Emerald is green," Bart explained to his buddies.

"She was really pretty," I added. "She looked like a model."

"Do you hear *that?"* Bart turned to his friends triumphantly. "I *told* you Velvet was really something."

As I walked back to our table, Daphne whispered, "That was a wonderful performance. I'm proud of you."

Patti Rogers stopped by to tell us the latest news. Everybody was laughing about Vonna's sneezing fit during the play. Vonna and her mother were having a terrible argument about it in the ladies' room. Mrs. Peckham claimed Vonna was allergic to the roses Bart had gotten for Velvet. Vonna claimed she was allergic to the makeup at the cosmetic salon her mother had taken her to.

Either way, it was poetic justice.

[illegible] waitress came over to take our order. "Is